Henning Mankell

AN EVENT IN AUTUMN

Henning Mankell's novels have been translated into forty languages and have sold more than forty million copies worldwide. He is the first winner of the Ripper Award (the new European prize for crime fiction) and has also received the Glass Key and Golden Dagger awards. His Kurt Wallander mysteries have been adapted into a PBS television series starring Kenneth Branagh. Mankell divides his time between Sweden and Mozambique.

www.henningmankell.com

AN EVENT
IN AUTUMN

A Kurt Wallander Mystery

Henning Mankell

*Translated from the Swedish
by Laurie Thompson*

Vintage Crime/Black Lizard
Vintage Books
A Division of Random House LLC
New York

A VINTAGE CRIME/BLACK LIZARD ORIGINAL, AUGUST 2014

Translation © 2013 by Laurie Thompson

The Cataloging-in-Publication Data is on file at the Library of Congress.

Vintage Trade Paperback ISBN: 978-0-8041-7064-2
eBook ISBN: 978-0-8041-7065-9

www.vintagebooks.com

www.henningmankell.com

Printed in the United States of America
10   9   8   7   6   5   4   3   2   1

AN EVENT IN AUTUMN

CHAPTER 1

On Saturday, October 26, 2002, Kurt Wallander woke up feeling very tired. It had been a trying week, as a severe cold had infected practically everybody in the Ystad police station. Wallander was usually the first to catch such viruses, but for some strange reason on this occasion he had been one of the few who did not fall ill. Since there had been a serious rape case in Svarte and several cases of GBH in Ystad during the week, Wallander had been forced to work long and strenuous hours.

He had remained at his desk until the early hours. He had been too exhausted to work, but at the same time he had no desire to go home to his apartment in Mariagatan. A squally wind was blowing hard outside the police station. Occasionally someone would walk along the corridor past his office, but Wallander hoped nobody would knock on his door. He wanted to be left in peace.

In peace from what? he asked himself. Perhaps what I want most of all is not to have to think about myself. About the increasing feeling of repugnance I'm carrying around inside myself and which I don't discuss with anybody else at all.

Autumn leaves swirled against the window of his office. He wondered if he ought to take some of the holiday owed to him and try to find a cheap package trip to Mallorca or some similar place. But he stopped short of making any such decision—even if the sun was shining down on a Spanish island, he would be unable to be at peace with himself.

He looked at his desk calendar. It was 2002. October. He had been a police officer for over thirty years, and had progressed from a probationer patrolling the streets of Malmö to become an experienced and respected detective who had successfully solved numerous difficult cases of serious crime. Even if he could not be pleased with his life as a human being, he could be pleased with his performance as a police officer. He had done his job well, and perhaps helped people to feel more secure.

A car in the street outside roared past at full speed, tires screaming. A young man at the wheel, Wallander thought. He is no doubt well aware that he is driving past the police station. His intention is to irritate us, of course. But he can't do that to me. Not anymore.

Wallander went out into the corridor. It was empty. He could hear faint sounds of laughter from behind a closed door. He went to fetch a cup of tea, then returned to his office.

The tea tasted odd. When he looked at the bag he realized that he had taken one tasting of sweet jasmine. He didn't like it, threw the bag into the wastepaper basket and poured the drink into a plant pot containing an orchid given to him by his daughter Linda.

It suddenly struck him how everything had changed during his many years as a police officer. When he had first started to patrol the streets there was a big difference between what happened in a city like Malmö and in small towns like Ystad. But nowadays there was hardly any difference at all. This was especially true for all the crimes connected with drugs. During his early days in Ystad a lot of drug addicts went to Copenhagen in order to obtain certain types of narcotic. Now you could buy everything in Ystad. He knew that there had also been an explosion in drug trafficking over the Internet.

Wallander often talked to his colleagues about how it had become so much more difficult to be a police officer in recent years. But now, as he sat in his office and watched the autumn leaves sticking onto the windowpane, he suddenly wondered if that were really true. Was that just an excuse? To avoid thinking about how society had changed, and hence also criminality?

Nobody has ever accused me of being lazy, Wallander

thought. But perhaps that's what I am, despite everything. Or am becoming so.

He stood up, put on the jacket that had been draped over his visitor chair, and left the office. His thoughts remained inside the room, the questions unanswered.

He drove home through the dark streets. Rainwater was glistening on the asphalt. His head was suddenly empty.

He had the next day off. Half asleep, he heard the distant ring of the telephone in the kitchen. His daughter Linda, who had started work as a police officer in Ystad the previous autumn, after finishing her training at the police college in Stockholm, was still living in his apartment. She should really have moved out by now, but had not yet received a contract for the apartment she had been promised. He heard her answer, and was relieved that he wouldn't need to bother about it. Martinson had recovered and been on duty since the previous day, and he had promised not to disturb Wallander.

Nobody else ever phoned him, especially not early on a Sunday morning. On the other hand, Linda spent ages every day on her cell phone. He had sometimes wondered about that. His own relationship with telephones was quite complicated. He felt put out whenever a phone rang. He guessed it was a sign of the simple truth that they belonged to different generations.

The bedroom door opened. He gave a start and became angry.

"Shouldn't you knock?"

"It's only me."

"What would you say if I flung open the door of your room without knocking?"

"I keep my door locked. You're wanted on the phone."

"Nobody ever rings me."

"But someone has."

"Who?"

"Martinson."

Wallander sat up in bed. Linda looked disapprovingly at his bare stomach, but said nothing. It was Sunday. They had made an agreement to the effect that for as long as she lived in his apartment, Sundays would be an exclusion zone in which neither of them was allowed to criticize the other. Sunday was proclaimed a day reserved for friendliness.

"What did he want?"

"He didn't say."

"Today is my day off."

"I don't know what he wants."

"Can't you tell him I'm out?"

"For God's sake!"

She left him and returned to her own room. Wallander shuffled out into the kitchen and picked up the telephone receiver. He could see through the window that it was raining, but the clouds were scattered and he could detect traces of blue sky.

"I thought today was supposed to be my day off!"

"So it is," said Martinson.

"What's happened?"

"Nothing."

Wallander noticed that he was becoming irritated again. Was Martinson ringing without any specific reason? That wasn't like him.

"Why are you ringing? I was asleep."

"Why do you sound so angry?"

"Because I *am* angry."

"I think I might have a house for you. Out in the countryside. Not so far from Löderup."

For many years Wallander had been thinking that it was high time he moved from his flat in central Ystad. He wanted to get out into the countryside, he wanted to acquire a dog. Since his father had died several years ago and Linda had flown the nest, he had felt an increasing need to change the circumstances of his own life. On several occasions he had been to view houses that real estate agents had on offer, but he had never found one to fulfill his requirements. Sometimes he had felt that the house was more or less right, but the price was out of his reach. His salary and his savings were inadequate. Being a police officer meant that a fat bank account was just not possible.

"Are you still there?"

"Yes, I'm still here. Tell me more."

"I can't just now. It seems there's been a break-in at the Åhléns supermarket last night. But if you drop by the station I can tell you about it. And I can let you have some keys."

Martinson hung up. Linda came into the kitchen and poured a cup of coffee. She looked inquiringly at her dad, then poured one for him as well. They sat down at the kitchen table.

"Do you have to work?"

"No."

"What did he want, then?"

"He wanted to show me a house."

"But he lives in a terraced house. You want to live out in the countryside, don't you?"

"You're not listening to what I say. He wants to show me a house. Not *his* house."

"What kind of a house?"

"I've no idea. Do you want to come with me?"

She shook her head. "No, I have other plans."

He didn't ask her what those plans were. He knew that she was the same as he was. She explained no more than was necessary. A question that wasn't asked was a question that didn't need an answer.

CHAPTER 2

Shortly after noon Wallander left for the police station. When he came out into the street he paused for a moment, wondering if he should take the car. But his conscience immediately began to nag him: he didn't get enough exercise. Besides, Linda was no doubt standing at the window, watching him. If he took the car, he'd never hear the last of it.

He started walking.

We're like an old married couple, he thought. Or a middle-aged policeman with much too young a wife. At first I was married to her mother. Now it's as if the two of us are living in some sort of strange marriage, my daughter and I. All very respectable. But a cause of mutual and constantly increasing irritation.

Martinson was sitting in his office when Wallander arrived at the deserted police station. While his colleague concluded a telephone call about a missing tractor, Wallander glanced through a new edict from the National Police Board that was lying on the desk. It was about the use of pepper spray. An experimental operation had taken place in southern Sweden recently, and an assessment had concluded that the weapon had proved to be an excellent device for calming down violent individuals.

Wallander suddenly felt old. He was a terrible shot and was always frightened of getting into a situation when he would be forced to fire his service pistol. It had happened, and a few years ago he had shot and killed a man in self-defense. But the very thought of expanding his limited arsenal with a collection of little cans of spray was not something he found attractive.

I'm growing too old, he thought. Too old for my own good, and too old for my job.

Martinson slammed down the receiver and jumped up from his chair. The action reminded Wallander of the young man who had joined the Ystad police some fifteen years earlier. Even then Martinson had been unsure whether or not he was cut out to be a police officer. On several occasions over the years he had been on the point of resigning—but he had always stayed on. Now he was no longer young. But unlike Wallander, he had not put on weight: on the contrary, he had grown thinner.

The biggest change was that his thick brown hair had vanished—Martinson had become bald.

Martinson gave him a bunch of keys. Wallander could see that most of them looked rather ancient.

"It belongs to a cousin of my wife's," said Martinson. "He's very old, the house is empty, but for ages he's been digging in his heels and refusing to sell it. Now he's in a care home, and he accepts that he won't be leaving there alive. A while ago he asked me to look after the selling of his house. The time has now come. I thought of you straightaway."

Martinson gestured toward a worn-out and rickety visitor chair. Wallander sat down.

"I thought of you for several reasons," he continued. "Partly because I knew you were looking for a house out in the country. But also because of where it's actually situated."

Wallander waited for what was coming next. He knew that Martinson had a tendency to make a long story of things—to complicate matters that ought to be simple.

"The house is in Vretsvägen, out in Löderup," said Martinson.

Wallander knew where he meant.

"Which house is it?"

"My wife's cousin is called Karl Eriksson."

Wallander thought for a moment.

"Wasn't he the one who had a smithy next to the gas station some years ago?"

"Yes, that's him."

Wallander stood up.

"I've driven past that house lots of times. It might be too close to where my father used to live for it to be suitable for me."

"Why not go and take a look?"

"How much does he want for it?"

"He's left that up to me. But as it's my wife who's in line for the money, I have to ask for a fair market price."

Wallander paused in the doorway. He had suddenly become doubtful.

"Could you perhaps give some indication of the asking price? There's not much point in my driving out there and looking at the house if it's going to be so expensive that I can't even contemplate buying it."

"Go and have a look," said Martinson. "You can afford it. If you want it."

CHAPTER 3

Wallander walked back to Mariagatan. He felt exhilarated, but also doubtful. Just as he got into the car it started pouring down. He drove out of Ystad, joined the Österleden motorway, and it occurred to him that it had been many years since he had last taken this route.

How long had his father been dead now? It took him some time to recall the year of his death. It was a long time ago. Many years had passed since they made that final journey together to Rome.

He recalled following his father, who had sneaked off to wander around Rome on his own. Wallander still felt a bit ashamed of having spied on him. The fact that his father was old and not fully in control of his senses was not a sufficient excuse. Why hadn't he left his father in peace to look around Rome and soak up his memories? Why had Wallander insisted on following him?

It wasn't good enough to say that he'd been concerned about his father, worried that something might have happened. Wallander could still recall his emotions from that time. He hadn't been especially worried. He had simply been curious.

Now, it was as if time had shrunk. Surely it could have been only yesterday that he drove out here to visit his father, to play cards with him, maybe have a drink and then start quarreling about something of no significance.

I miss the old man, Wallander thought. He was the only father I'll ever have. He was often a pain in the neck and could drive me up the wall. But I miss him. There's no getting away from that.

Wallander turned off into a familiar road and glimpsed the roof of his father's old house. But he continued past the side road and turned in the other direction instead.

He stopped after two hundred meters and got out of the car. It was only drizzling now.

Karl Eriksson's house was in a neglected and overgrown garden. It was an old Scanian farmhouse, and would originally have had two wings. One had disappeared—maybe it had burned down, maybe it had been demolished. The house and garden were well away from the road, apparently in the middle of a field. The soil had been tilled, and was waiting for its winter covering of snow and ice. In the distance Wallander could hear the noise of a tractor.

Wallander opened the squeaking gate and entered the yard. The sandy path had certainly not been raked for many years. A small flock of crows was cawing away in a tall chestnut tree directly in front of the house. Perhaps it was originally the family's magic tree—planted in the old days to stand guard over the house and be a home to the trolls and fairies and spirits who looked after the welfare of the inhabitants. Wallander stood still underneath it and listened—he needed to like the noise surrounding a house before he could start thinking about the possibility of living in it. If the sound of the wind or even the silence wasn't right, he might just as well get back in his car and drive away. But he was duly impressed by what he heard. It was the stillness of autumn, the Scanian autumn, waiting for the onset of winter.

Wallander walked around the building. Behind it were a few apple trees, currant bushes and some dilapidated stone tables, chairs and benches. He strolled around among the fallen autumn leaves, stumbling over something lying on the ground—possibly the remains of an old rake—and returned to the front of the house. He guessed which of the keys would open the front door, inserted it in the keyhole and turned it.

The house was musty and stuffy inside and there was a distinct smell of old man. He explored the rooms one by one. The furniture was old-fashioned and worn; crocheted proverbs hung on the walls. An ancient television set stood in what must have been the old man's bedroom. Wallander went into the kitchen. There was a refrigerator that had been switched off. In the sink were the remains of a dead mouse. He went upstairs, but the upper floor was simply an unfurnished loft. The house would need a lot of work, that was obvious. And it wouldn't be cheap, even if he were able to do much of it himself.

He returned downstairs, sat down cautiously on an old sofa, and dialed the number of the Ystad police station. It was several minutes before Martinson answered.

"Where are you?" Martinson asked.

"In the old days people used to ask how you were," said Wallander. "Now they ask where you are. The way we greet each other really has undergone a revolution."

"Did you ring me in order to tell me that?"

"I'm sitting inside the house."

"What do you think?"

"I don't know. It feels unfamiliar."

"But it's the first time you've been there, isn't it? Of course it feels unfamiliar."

"I'd like to know what kind of price you're asking for it. I don't want to start thinking seriously about it until I know that. I take it you know there's a lot of work that needs doing."

"I've been there. I know that."

Wallander waited. He could hear Martinson breathing.

"It's not easy to do business with good friends," said Martinson eventually. "I can see that now."

"Regard me as an enemy," said Wallander cheerfully. "But preferably a poverty-stricken enemy."

Martinson laughed.

"We've been thinking in terms of a bargain price. Five hundred thousand. No haggling."

Wallander had already decided that he could pay a maximum of 550,000.

"That's too expensive," he said.

"The hell it is! For a house in much sought-after Österlen?"

"The place is a ramshackle hovel."

"If you spend a hundred thousand on it, it will be worth well over a million."

"I can stretch to four hundred and seventy-five thousand."

"No."

"That's that, then."

Wallander hung up. Then he stood with the cell phone in his hand, waiting. Counting the seconds. He got as far as twenty-four before Martinson rang.

"Let's say four hundred and ninety thousand."

"Let's shake on that over the phone," said Wallander. "Or rather, I'll pay a deposit twenty-four hours from now. I need to talk to Linda first."

"Do that, then. And say yea or nay by this evening."

"Why the rush? I need twenty-four hours."

"OK, you can have them. But no more."

They ended the call. Wallander felt a surge of elation. Was he now, at long last, about to acquire the house in the country he had dreamed about for so long? And in the vicinity of his father's house, where he had spent so much time?

He worked his way through the house once more. In his mind's eye he was already knocking down partition walls, installing new electricity sockets, papering the walls, buying furniture. He was tempted to phone Linda, but managed to control himself.

It was too early to tell her. He still wasn't totally convinced.

He walked around the ground floor once again, pausing here and there to listen before continuing into the next room. Hanging on the walls were faded photographs of the people who used to live there. Between two windows in the biggest room was also a colored aerial photograph of the house and grounds.

He thought about the possibility of people who had once lived there still being present and breathing in the walls. But there are no ghosts here, he thought. There aren't any because I don't believe in ghosts.

Wallander went out into the garden. It had stopped raining, and the clouds were dispersing. He pushed and pulled the handle of a pump in the middle of the courtyard. There were squeaking and grinding noises, and the water that eventually appeared was first brown, but then turned crystal clear. He tasted it, and found himself already imagining a dog drinking water from a bowl by his side.

He walked around the outside of the house one more time, then returned to the car.

Just after opening the car door he paused: a thought had struck him. At first he couldn't understand what it was that was preventing him from sitting down behind the steering wheel. He frowned. Something was nagging away inside him. Something he had seen. Something that didn't fit in.

He turned to face the house. Something or other had etched itself into his brain.

Then it dawned on him. He had stumbled over something lying on the ground at the back of the house. The remains of a small rake, or perhaps the root of a tree. That was what was preventing him from leaving the place.

It was something he had seen. Without seeing it properly.

CHAPTER 4

Wallander returned to the back of the house. At first he couldn't be sure exactly where he had stumbled, nor could he understand why he seemed to think it was so important to find out what it was that had nearly tripped him up.

He looked around, and before long found what he was looking for. He stared long and hard at the object that was sticking up out of the ground. At first he just stood there motionless, but then he walked slowly around it. When he returned to his starting point Wallander squatted down. His knees felt stiff.

There was no question about what was lying there, half buried in the soil. It was not the remains of an old rake. Nor was it a tree root.

It was a hand. The bones were brown, but there was no doubt in his mind. It was the remains of a human hand, sticking up out of the brown clay soil.

Wallander straightened up. The alarm bell that had started ringing when he had stood there with his hand on the handle of the car door had delivered him a serious warning.

There was no sign of other bones. Just that hand sticking up out of the ground. He bent down again and poked cautiously into the earth. Was there a whole skeleton under there, or was it just the hand? He was unable to decide for sure.

The clouds had disappeared. The October sun was giving a suggestion of warmth. The crows were still cawing away in the tall chestnut tree. The whole situation seemed to Wallander to be unreal. He'd driven out on a Sunday to take a look at a house he might decide to move into. And, purely by chance, he had happened upon human remains in the garden.

Wallander shook his head in disbelief. Then he phoned the police station. Martinson was in no hurry to answer.

"I'm not going to reduce the price any further. My wife thinks I've gone too far already."

"It's got nothing to do with the price."

"What's it about, then?"

"Come here and see."

"Has something happened?"

"Come here. Just do that. Come here."

Martinson realized that something important must have happened. He asked no more questions. Wallander continued walking around the garden, scrutinizing the ground while he waited for the police car to turn up. It took nineteen minutes. Martinson had driven fast. Wallander met him in front of the house. Martinson seemed worried.

"What's happened?"

"I stumbled."

Martinson looked at him in surprise.

"Did you ring me just to say that you'd stumbled over something?"

"In a way, yes. I want you to see what it was that I stumbled over."

They walked around to the back of the house. Wallander pointed. Martinson stepped back in surprise.

"What the hell is that?"

"It looks like a hand. Obviously I can't tell if there's a whole skeleton."

Martinson continued to stare at the hand in astonishment.

"I don't understand a thing."

"A hand is a hand. A dead hand is a dead person's hand. As this isn't a cemetery, there's something odd here."

They stood there, staring at the hand. Wallander wondered what Martinson was thinking. Then he wondered what he was thinking himself.

The desire to buy this house had deserted him altogether.

CHAPTER 5

Two hours later the whole house and grounds had been sealed off by police tape, and the technical team had started work. Martinson had tried to persuade Wallander to go home, as it was his day off, but Wallander had no intention of following Martinson's advice. His Sunday was already ruined.

Wallander wondered what would have happened if he hadn't stumbled over the hand. If he had bought the house and only later discovered the human bones. How would he react if it turned out that there was a whole skeleton lying in the ground?

A police officer buys a house from a colleague, then discovers that a serious crime of violence has been committed on the premises. He could imagine the newspapers and their sensationalist headlines.

The forensic pathologist, who had come from Lund, was called Stina Hurlén and in Wallander's opinion was far too young for the job she was doing. But he said nothing, of course. Besides, in her favor was that she paid meticulous attention to detail.

Martinson and Wallander waited while Hurlén made a quick preliminary investigation. Nyberg, the officer in charge of the forensic team, could be heard complaining angrily in the background. Wallander had the feeling he had heard similar rants a thousand times before. On this occasion the problem was a missing tarpaulin.

It's always missing, he thought. During all my years as a police officer a damned tarpaulin has always been mislaid.

Stina Hurlén stood up.

"Well, it's a human hand all right. An adult's hand. Not a child's."

"How long has it been lying there?"

"I don't know."

"Surely you must have some idea?"

"You know how I hate guessing. And besides, I'm not a specialist in pieces of bones."

Wallander eyed her in silence for a moment.

"Let's take a guess. I'll guess and you'll guess. As we don't know. The guesses might help us to get started. Even if they eventually turn out to be quite wrong."

Hurlén thought for a moment.

"All right, I'll take a guess," she said. "I might be completely wrong, but I think that hand has been lying there for a long time."

"Why do you think that?"

"I don't know. I don't even really think it—I'm only guessing. Perhaps you could say that experience is set on autopilot."

Wallander left her to sort herself out and went over to Martinson, who was speaking on his cell phone. He had a mug of coffee in his other hand. He held it out toward Wallander. Neither of them took milk or sugar with their coffee. Wallander took a sip. Martinson hung up.

"Hurlén thinks the hand has been lying here for a long time."

"Hurlén?"

"The pathologist. Haven't you come across her before?"

"Huh, they're changing all the time in Lund. What's happened to all the old pathologists? They just seem to disappear into their own private heaven."

"Wherever they all are, Hurlén thinks the hand has been lying here for a long time. That could mean anything, of course. But maybe you know something about the history of this house?"

"Not a lot. Karl Eriksson has owned it for about thirty years. But I don't know who he bought it from."

They went into the house and sat down at the kitchen table. Wallander had the feeling that he was now in a house quite different from the one he had come to look at a couple of hours earlier, wondering whether to buy it or not.

"I suppose we'll have to dig up the whole garden," said Martinson. "But I gather that they first have to check it out with a new machine—some sort of detector for human remains. A bit like a metal detector. Nyberg has no faith in it at all, but his boss insists. I reckon Nyberg is looking forward to the fancy new machine turning out to be useless, so that he can resort to his tried and tested method of digging away with spades."

"What happens if we don't find anything?"

Martinson frowned. "What do you mean?"

"What do you think I mean? There's a hand lying there in the ground. That suggests there ought to be more hidden away down there. A whole body. Let's face it, how can a dead hand come flying into this garden? Has a crow found it somewhere and then happened to drop it here of all places? Do hands grow in this garden? Or has it been raining hands over Löderup this autumn?"

"You're right," said Martinson. "We ought to find more bones."

Wallander gazed out of the window, thinking hard.

"Nobody knows what we might find," he said. "Possibly a whole graveyard. An old plague cemetery perhaps?"

They went out into the garden again. Martinson spoke to Nyberg and some of the other technicians. Wallander thought about his imaginary dog, which just then seemed more unlikely than ever.

Martinson and Wallander drove back to the police station. They parked their cars and went to Martinson's office, which was in a bigger mess than Wallander had ever seen it before. Once upon a time, a long time ago, Martinson had been an extremely well-organized, almost pedantic police officer. Now he lived in a state of chaos, in which anybody would think it was impossible to find a particular document at all.

Martinson seemed to have read his thoughts.

"It looks a hell of a mess in here," he said grimly, removing several papers from his desk chair. "I try to keep it tidy, but no matter what I do the papers and files just keep on piling up."

"It's the same with me," said Wallander. "When I first managed to work out how to use a computer, I thought the heaps of paper would dwindle away. Some hope— things just got even worse."

He gazed out of the window.

"Go home," said Martinson. "This is your day off. I feel terrible about asking you to take a look at that house."

"I liked it," said Wallander. "I liked it and I was pretty sure that Linda would have been just as enthusiastic. I'd already made up my mind to phone you and confirm that I was going to buy it. Now I'm not so sure."

Martinson accompanied him down to reception.

"Just what is it we've found?" said Wallander. "A hand. The remains of a hand. In a garden."

He broke off as he didn't need to say any more. They had a case of murder to solve. Unless the hand had been lying there for so long that it would be impossible to identify it or establish the cause of death.

"I'll phone you," said Martinson. "If nothing happens, I'll see you tomorrow."

"At eight o'clock," said Wallander. "We'll have a run-through then. If I know Nyberg he'll spend all night digging away out there."

Martinson returned to his office. Wallander got into his car, then changed his mind and left it parked where it was. He walked back home, taking the long route through town and pausing at the kiosk next to the railway station where he bought an evening newspaper.

The clouds were gathering again.

He also noticed that it was getting colder.

CHAPTER 6

Wallander opened the front door and listened. Linda wasn't at home. He made some tea and sat down at the kitchen table. The discovery of the hand had disappointed him. For a brief time during his visit to the house, he had been convinced: it was exactly the place he had been looking for. That house and no other. But then its garden had been transformed into a crime scene. Or, at least, somewhere concealing a dark secret.

I shall never find a house, he thought. No house, no dog, no new woman either. Everything will remain the same as it always has been.

He drank his tea then went to lie down on the bed. As it was Sunday, he ought to comply with the routine—

a routine introduced by Linda—and change the sheets. But he didn't have the strength.

When he woke up he found he had been asleep for several hours. It was pitch-black outside. Linda still hadn't come home. He went into the kitchen and drank some water. As he placed the glass on the draining board, the telephone rang.

"Wallander."

"It's Nyberg here. We're waiting."

"Waiting for what?"

"For you. What do you think?"

"Why are you waiting for me?"

Nyberg sighed profoundly. Wallander could hear that he was tired and irritated.

"Hasn't the switchboard rung you?"

"Nobody has rung here."

"How the hell can it be possible to carry out police work when you can't even rely on various messages being passed on?"

"Never mind that now. What's happened?"

"We've found a body."

"A body or a skeleton?"

"What do you think? A skeleton, of course."

"I'll be there."

Wallander replaced the receiver, selected a sweater from the wardrobe and scribbled a note, which he placed on the kitchen table. *Gone to work.* He hurried to the police station and collected his car. When he got there and felt in his pocket for the key, he remembered that he had put it on the kitchen table.

For a brief moment he felt like crying. Or just walking away from it all, without turning back. Walking away never to return.

He felt like an idiot. An idiot he felt sorry for, just for a moment. Then he went over to one of the patrol cars and asked them to drive him out to the house. His self-pity had faded away and been replaced by anger. Somebody had failed to inform him that he had needed to drive out to Löderup.

He leaned back in the car seat, listening to the various messages coming through over the police radio. The image of his father suddenly appeared in his thoughts.

Once upon a time he'd had a father. But one day he passed away, and the urn with his ashes had been buried in the cemetery. And now, in a flash, the time that had passed since then had been erased. It was as if it had happened the previous day. Or had merely been a dream.

The garden was illuminated by strong spotlights. Every time Wallander went to a crime scene at night, when work was in progress, he had the feeling that he was on a film set.

Nyberg came toward him. The forensic officer was covered in soil and clay from top to toe—Nyberg's filthy overalls were so well known that they had once been featured in an article in the local newspaper.

"I don't know why you weren't informed," he said. Wallander made a dismissive gesture.

"It doesn't matter. What have you found?"

"I've already told you."

"A skeleton?"

"Exactly."

Wallander accompanied Nyberg to a spot close to where he had stumbled in the first instance. There was now a hole, just over a meter deep. In it were the remains of a person. In addition to the skeleton, which seemed to be more or less intact, there were a few scraps of clothing.

Wallander walked around the corpse. Nyberg coughed and blew his nose. Martinson came out of the house, yawned—and looked at Wallander, who said nothing until he had completed his inspection of the skeleton.

"Where's Hurlén?"

"She had just gone home," said Nyberg ironically. "But I phoned her when we started to find several bones. She'll be back here soon."

Wallander and Martinson crouched down.

"Man or woman?"

It was Martinson who asked the question. Wallander had learned over the years that the easiest way of distinguishing between the skeleton of a man and a woman was by examining the pelvis. But what exactly was it he should be looking for? He found that he could no longer remember.

"A man," he said. "At least, I hope it's a man."

Martinson looked at him in surprise.

"Why?"

"I don't know. I suppose I don't like the thought of thinking about buying a house with a dead woman lying in the garden."

Wallander's knees creaked as he stood up.

"One wonders about that hand," he said. "Why did it suddenly start poking up out of the ground?"

"Perhaps it wanted to wave to us and tell us there was something hidden away under the ground that shouldn't be there."

Martinson was well aware that his comment sounded idiotic. But Wallander said nothing.

Stina Hurlén suddenly appeared under the spotlights. There was a squelching sound as her rubber boots tramped their way over the downtrodden soil. She did the same as Wallander had done, and walked around the hole before crouching.

"Man or woman?" asked Wallander.

"Woman," said Hurlén. "Definitely a woman. No doubt about it. But don't ask me about her age, or anything else come to that. I'm too tired to start guessing."

"Just one more thing," said Martinson. "You thought before that the hand had been lying here for a long time. Does the discovery of the skeleton change that opinion? Or do you still think she's been lying here for ages?"

"I don't think. My guess is she's been here for a long time."

"Can you see anything that might indicate the cause of her death?" asked Martinson.

"That was question number two," said Hurlén. "One question too many. You're not going to get an answer."

"That hand," said Wallander. "Why is it sticking up?"

"That's not unusual," answered Nyberg when Hurlén remained silent. "Things lying in the ground move around. It can be due to differences in groundwater levels. And besides, this is Scanian clay soil—subsidence takes place. Personally I think the hand came up to the surface as a result of all the rain we've had this autumn. But of course it could also have been field mice."

Nyberg's cell phone rang. He did not conclude his analysis of why the hand had stuck up through the earth.

"What do you think he meant?" wondered Martinson. "That reference to field mice?"

"I've always thought that Nyberg is a brilliant forensic officer. But I've also always been convinced that he's hopeless when it comes to explaining what he means."

"I'm going home to get some sleep," said Martinson. "I think you ought to do that as well. There's not much we can do here in any case."

Martinson drove Wallander home. As usual, he drove very jerkily; but Wallander said nothing. He had given up many years ago. Martinson drove in a way that would never change.

CHAPTER 7

Linda was still up and about when Wallander came in through the door. She was in her dressing gown, and eyed his muddy shoes. They sat down in the kitchen and he told her what had happened.

"That sounds very strange," she said when he had finished. "A house Martinson tipped you off about? And there's a dead body buried in the garden?"

"It may sound strange, but it's true."

"Who is it?"

"How the hell can we be expected to know that?"

"Why do you sound so angry?"

"I'm tired. And maybe disappointed as well. I liked that house. And I could have managed the price."

She reached out her hand and tapped him on the arm.

"There are other houses," she said. "And you do have a home already, of course."

"I suppose I was disappointed," said Wallander again. "I could have done with a bit of good news, today of all days. Not a bit of a skeleton sticking out of the ground."

"Can't you try to see it as something exciting? Instead of a boring old garden, you get something that nobody knows about."

"I don't understand what you mean."

Linda looked at him in amusement.

"You wouldn't need to risk being burgled," she said. "I think thieves are just as scared of ghosts as everybody else is."

Wallander put the kettle on. Linda shook her head when he asked her if she'd like some tea.

He sat down with a pink teacup.

"You got that from me," said Linda. "Do you remember?"

"You gave me it as a Christmas present when you were eight years old," he said. "And I've always drunk tea out of this cup ever since."

"It cost one krona at a rummage sale."

Wallander sipped the tea. Linda yawned.

"I was looking forward to living in that house," he said. "Or at least I'd begun to believe that I could move out of town at long last."

"There are other houses," said Linda.

"It's not as easy as that."

"What's so difficult about it?"

"I think I demand too much."

"Demand a bit less then!"

Wallander could feel that he was beginning to get angry again. Ever since she had been in her teens, Linda had accused him of making his life more complicated than it needed to be. He knew that what irritated him most of all was that, on occasions like this, Linda reminded him of her mother. And her voice was almost identical to Mona's. If Wallander closed his eyes he felt uncertain about who was actually sitting opposite him at the kitchen table.

"Enough of that now," said Wallander, rinsing out his cup.

"I'm going to bed," said Linda.

Wallander sat up for a while, watching the television with the sound turned down. One of the channels was showing a program about penguins.

He woke up with a start. It was four o'clock in the morning. The television was blank but buzzing. He switched it off and hurried to bed before he had time to wake up properly.

CHAPTER 8

It was two minutes past eight on Monday, October 28, when Wallander closed the door of one of the police station's conference rooms behind him. He had slept badly after waking up on the sofa. And to make things worse, his electric razor had broken. He was unshaven and felt dirty. Sitting around the table were the people he was used to working alongside. He had been working with some of them for over fifteen years. It occurred to him that these were people who made up the content of a large proportion of his life. He was now the one who had been working longer than anybody else in the Ystad CID. Once upon a time he'd been the newcomer.

Those present at the meeting, apart from Wallander

himself, were Nyberg, Martinson and the chief of police, Lisa Holgersson. She was the first female boss Wallander had worked for. When she first came to Ystad some time in the 1990s, he had been as skeptical as all the other—mainly male—officers. But he had soon realized that Lisa Holgersson was very competent. It became clear to him that she might well be the best boss he had ever had. Over the years that ensued he had found no reason to reconsider that judgment, even if they had occasionally had fierce disagreements.

Wallander took a deep breath and turned first to Nyberg, then to Martinson, who had spoken to Stina Hurlén before the meeting.

Nyberg was tired and looked at Wallander with blood-shot eyes. He ought to have retired by now, but he had changed his mind and stayed on. Wallander was not surprised. Despite all the unpleasant aspects of his work, without it Nyberg would find life pointless.

"A dead body," said Nyberg. "A few decayed scraps of clothing. It's not my job to look for the cause of death among all the old bones, but nothing seemed to be broken or crushed. I haven't found anything else. The question is, of course, whether we should dig up the whole garden."

"How did that new machine perform?" asked Holgersson.

"Exactly as I thought it would," growled Nyberg. "It's a bundle of crap that some idiot has tricked the Swedish police into buying. Why can't we have a dog trained to sniff out corpses?"

Wallander found it hard not to burst out laughing. Even if Nyberg could be surly and difficult to work with, he had a unique sense of humor. He also had views that Wallander shared.

"Stina Hurlén needs a bit of time," said Martinson, leafing through his notebook. "The bones have to be examined. But she thought she would be able to give us some kind of report later today."

Wallander nodded. "So, that's all we have to go on so far," he said. "It's not a lot—but of course we have to face up to the possibility that this might become a murder inquiry. For the moment, we have to wait for what Stina Hurlén has to say. What we can start doing right away is to see if we can dig out something about the history of the house and the people who have lived there. Has there been a missing person linked with the house? That's a question we can ask ourselves. As Martinson has a relative who owns the house, perhaps he ought to be the one to look after that aspect."

Wallander placed his hands down on the table to indicate that the meeting was closed. Lisa Holgersson held him back as the others left the room.

"The media want to talk to you," she said.

"We've found a skeleton. There's nothing more to say."

"You know that journalists love stories about missing persons. Isn't there anything else you can tell them?"

"No. We police officers have to wait until we get more facts. The journalists can jolly well do the same."

Wallander spent the rest of the day on an inquiry concerning a Pole who had beaten and killed an Ystad resident at some drunken orgy or other. A lot of people had been there at the time, but they all remembered it differently—or had no recollection of it at all. The Polish man who was accused of killing his drinking partner kept changing his story. Wallander had spent hours on fruitless conversations with those involved, and had asked the prosecutor if it was really worth continuing. But the prosecutor was young and new and assiduous, and had insisted. A man, drunk or not, who had killed another man, even if he was just as drunk, must be duly punished. Wallander couldn't argue with that, of course. But his experience told him that they would never be able to throw light on the situation, no matter how long he or one of his colleagues persisted with the inquiry.

Martinson called in occasionally to report that Stina Hurlén had still not been in touch. Shortly after two, Linda appeared in the doorway and asked if he was going out for lunch. He shook his head and asked her to buy him a sandwich instead. When she had left, he found himself thinking that he still hadn't managed to get used to the fact that his own daughter was now a fully grown adult, and a police officer to boot, working at the same police station as he was.

Linda duly delivered the sandwich in a small carrier bag. Wallander slid aside the voluminous file containing all the material relevant to the drunken orgy. He ate the sandwich, closed the door, then leaned back on his chair for a snooze. As usual he held his bunch of keys in one hand. If he dropped it, he would know he had fallen asleep and that it was time to wake up again.

He soon dozed off. The keys fell to the floor, and as they did so Martinson opened the door.

Wallander gathered that Stina Hurlén had sent in her report at last.

CHAPTER 9

The preliminary, but by no means final, forensic report had come from Lund by courier. It was lying on Martinson's desk.

"I think you'd better read it yourself," said Martinson.

"I take it that means the discovery of the skeleton is what we suspected it would be—the beginning of a criminal investigation."

"It seems so, yes."

Martinson went to get some coffee while Wallander read the report. Stina Hurlén wrote simply and clearly. Over the years Wallander had often wondered why police officers and pathologists, prosecutors and defense lawyers sometimes wrote such hopelessly unreadable texts. They turned out masses of words instead of writing simple, meaningful sentences.

It took him just over ten minutes to read the report. Whenever he had an important document in his hands, he forced himself to read slowly, at a speed all his thoughts could keep up with.

Stina Hurlén confirmed that the body was definitely that of a woman. She judged that the woman would have been about fifty when she died. Further analyses would be needed to be precise about her age, but Hurlén could already give the probable cause of death. The dead woman had been hanged. There was an injury on the nape of her neck which indicated this. Needless to say, Hurlén could not be certain that the injury hadn't been caused after her death, but she thought that was unlikely. As yet she was unable to say how long the woman had been dead, but there were indications that the corpse had been lying in the grave for many years.

Wallander put the report down on the desk and picked up the cup of coffee Martinson had brought him.

"What do we know then?" said Wallander. "If we sum up."

"Unusually little. A dead woman in a shallow grave in a garden in Löderup. Who was about fifty when she died. But we don't know when she died. If I understand Hurlén rightly, that woman could have been lying under the ground for a hundred years. Or more."

"Or less," said Wallander. "What's the name of the owner of the house? Your relative?"

"Karl Eriksson. My wife's cousin."

"I suppose the best we can do is to have a chat with him."

"No," said Martinson. "I don't think that's a very good idea."

"Why not?"

"He's ill. He's old."

"Being old doesn't mean being ill. What are you implying?"

Martinson walked over to the window and looked out.

"All I'm saying is that my wife's cousin Karl Eriksson is ninety-two years old. He was clear in the head until a few months ago, but then something happened. One day he went out into the street naked, and when people tried to help him he didn't know who he was or where he lived. He'd managed on his own at home until then. Dementia normally comes creeping up on you—but in his case it hit him with a bang."

Wallander looked at Martinson in surprise.

"But if he became senile so suddenly, how could he ask you to look after the sale of his house?"

"I've already told you. We drew up an agreement about that several years ago. Perhaps he had an inkling that one of these days he would float off into the mists, and wanted to have his affairs in order before it happened."

"Does he have any moments of clarity?"

"None at all. He doesn't recognize anybody anymore. The only person he ever talks about is his mother, who died about fifty years ago. He keeps saying he must go and buy some milk. He repeats that over and over again all the time he's awake. He lives in a care home for people who no longer live in the real world."

"Surely there must be someone else who can answer questions?"

"No, there isn't. Karl Eriksson and his wife, who died sometime in the 1970s, didn't have any children. Or rather, they had two children, two daughters, who died in a horrific accident in a muddy pond a long time ago. There were no other relatives. They lived isolated lives— the only people they were occasionally in contact with were me and my family."

Wallander felt impatient. And he was also hungry—the sandwich Linda had given him had long since proved insufficient.

"We'd better start searching the house," he said, rising to his feet. "There must be deeds. All people have a story; so do all houses. Let's go and have a word with Lisa."

They sat down in Lisa Holgersson's office. Wallander let Martinson tell her about Stina Hurlén's report and the senile Karl Eriksson. It had become a characteristic of their working relationship that they took it in turns to report on specific cases so that the other one could listen and keep the whole business at arm's length.

"We can't devote much in the way of resources to this," said Holgersson when Martinson had finished. "It seems highly probable that it will end up as an old murder inquiry in any case."

That was exactly the reaction that Wallander had expected. It seemed to him that in recent years fewer and fewer police resources were allocated to what ought to have been most important: fieldwork. More and more of his colleagues were glued to their desks, and had to work in accordance with confusing and meaningless priorities that were changing all the time. An old murder, if that was really what had come up to the surface in Löderup, was not something that could be allocated anything more than strictly limited resources.

He had expected that answer, but was angry even so.

"We'll keep you informed," he said. "We'll just say for the moment what we know, and that we think perhaps we ought to make a thorough investigation. We're not asking for much in the way of resources. At least, not until we receive more detailed reports from the Center for Forensic Medicine in Lund. And Nyberg's report. After all, that's the least we can do—find out who it is who's been lying there buried for years. If we still want to call ourselves police officers."

Lisa Holgersson gave a start and glared sternly at him.

"What did you mean by that last sentence?"

"It's the results of what we do that show we're police officers. Not all those statistics we're forced to spend time working out."

"Statistics?"

"You know as well as I do that our ability to clear up crime is much too limited. Because we're obliged to spend so much time messing around with unimportant paperwork."

Wallander could feel that he was on the verge of bursting into a fit of rage. But he managed to control himself sufficiently for Lisa Holgersson not to notice just how furious he actually was.

Martinson saw through him, of course.

Wallander stood up hastily.

"We'll go and take a look out there," he said, trying hard to maintain a friendly tone. "Who knows what we might find?"

He left the room and strode rapidly along the corridor. Martinson half ran behind him.

"I thought you were going to burst," said Martinson. "Not a good idea on a Monday in October as winter is approaching."

"You talk too much," said Wallander. "Fetch your jacket—we're going for a drive out into the sticks."

CHAPTER 10

When they arrived at the house in Löderup, nearly all the spotlights were switched off. The hole in which they had discovered the body was covered by a tarpaulin. A single police car was parked by the cordoned-off area; Nyberg and the other forensic officers had left. Wallander still had the house keys in his pocket. He handed them over to Martinson.

"I'm not out viewing houses now," he said. "These are your keys, so it's up to you to open up."

"Why does everything have to be so complicated?" asked Martinson.

He didn't wait for an answer. They entered the house and switched on the lights.

"Deeds," said Wallander. "Documents that tell the story

of the house. Let's devote some time to looking for those. Then we can wait until the forensic boys and the medical crowd have had their say."

"I asked Stefan to conduct a search through old reports on missing persons," said Martinson. "Linda was going to help him."

Stefan Lindman had joined the Ystad police at about the same time as Linda. Wallander soon realized that Linda and Stefan were involved in some kind of relationship. When he tried to talk to her about it, he had got mainly evasive responses. Wallander liked Stefan Lindman. He was a good police officer. But he found it hard to reconcile himself to the thought that he had a daughter who no longer regarded him as the most important man in her life.

They began their search at opposite ends of the house—Martinson in the bedroom and Wallander in what seemed to be a combination of drawing room and study.

Once he was alone, Wallander stood absolutely still for a moment and allowed his gaze and his thoughts to wander around the room. Had there once been a woman here who for some reason or other had been murdered and then buried in the garden? Why had nobody missed her if this had been where she lived? What had happened in this house, and when? Twenty years ago? Fifty years ago? Perhaps a hundred years ago?

Wallander started searching methodically. First with

his eyes. People always leave a lot of traces behind them. And he knew that people were hamsters. They kept things, not least documents. His eyes alighted on a desk in front of a window. That was where he would start. The desk was dark brown, definitely old. Wallander sat down on the chair in front of it and tried the drawers. They were locked. He searched the desk top but could see no sign of a key. Then he felt with his fingers underneath the desk top: still no keys. He lifted up the heavy, brass table lamp, and found a key attached to a thin strand of silk.

He opened the desk's cupboard. There were five drawers. The top one was full of old pens, empty ink bottles, a few pairs of spectacles, and dust. It struck Wallander that nothing could make him as depressed as the sight of old spectacles that nobody wanted anymore. He opened the next drawer down. It contained a bundle of old income tax returns. He saw that the oldest was from 1952. That year Karl Eriksson and his wife had paid 2,900 kronor in tax. Wallander tried to work out if that was about what might have been expected, or if it was a surprisingly low sum. He decided the latter. The third drawer contained various diaries. He leafed through some of them. They contained no personal notes, not even references to birthdays: just the purchase of seedcorn, the cost of repairs to a combine harvester, and new wheels for a tractor. Eriksson had evidently run a small farm. He put the diaries back into the drawer. Every time he searched through other people's belongings, he wondered how anybody could cope with being a thief—to spend more or less every day rummaging through other people's clothes and personal belongings.

Wallander opened the fourth drawer, the last but one. And there he found what he was looking for: a file with the words "Property Documents" written in ink. He took it carefully out of the drawer, slid the desk lamp closer to him, directed it at the file, and began to leaf through the papers. The first thing he came across was a deed of conveyance dated November 18, 1968. Karl Eriksson and his wife Emma had bought the property and the surrounding fields from the estate left by the farmer Gustav Valfrid Henander. The beneficiaries comprised the widow, Laura, and three children: Tore, Lars and Kristina. The purchase price was 55,000 kronor. Karl Eriksson paid a deposit of 15,000 kronor on the house, and the transaction was supervised by the Savings Bank in Ystad.

Wallander produced a notebook and pencil from his jacket pocket. In the old days he had nearly always forgotten to take a notebook with him, and been forced to scribble on scraps of paper and the backs of receipts. But Linda had bought him a collection of small notebooks, and put one in the pocket of each of his coats and jackets. Wallander made a note of two figures: at the top he wrote today's date, October 28, 2002, and underneath it, November 18, 1968. This was a stretch of time covering thirty-four years—a whole generation. He noted down all the names that were on the conveyance, then put it to one side and surveyed the remaining documents. Most of them were of no interest, but he proceeded carefully. Working through a series of documents could be just as risky as walking through a dark forest: you could stumble, fall down, get lost.

Martinson's cell phone rang somewhere. Wallander assumed it was his wife. They had innumerable phone conversations with each other every day. Wallander often wondered what they could possibly think of to say. He couldn't remember phoning his own wife Mona, or her him, during working hours even once over all the years they were married. Work was work, and talking was something you could do before or afterward. He sometimes wondered if that had been a contributory factor in the break-up of their marriage. The fact that he had phoned her so seldom. Or her him.

He carried on looking at the documents. Paused. He found he was holding an old title deed, an attested copy. It was dated 1949 and concerned Gustav Valfrid Henander. Henander had bought the property, Legshult 2:19, from Ludvig Hansson, who was listed as a widower and the sole owner. The purchase price had been 29,000 kronor, and this time the transaction was arranged by the Skurup Savings Bank.

Wallander noted it all down. Another few years were now accounted for. He had gone back in time fifty-three years from 2002. He smiled to himself. When Ludvig

Hansson had sold his farm to Gustav Valfrid Henander, Wallander was a little boy, still living in Limhamn. He had no memories from that time.

He carried on searching. Martinson had finished his call and was now whistling to himself. Wallander thought it was something Barbra Streisand had sung. Maybe "Woman in Love." Martinson was a good whistler. Wallander looked at some more documents, but there were none that went back further in time. Ludvig Hansson had left the property in 1949. The desk drawer contained no more answers to questions about what had happened before then.

He searched the rest of the room without finding anything of interest. Not even in a corner cupboard or a secretary.

Martinson came in, sat down in a chair and yawned. Wallander told him what he had found, but Martinson shook his head when he handed over the papers.

"I don't need to look. Ludvig Hansson. That name means nothing to me."

"We'll carry on looking via the land register," said Wallander. "Tomorrow. But at least we now have a sort of outline covering the last fifty years or so. Have you found anything?"

"No. A few photo albums. But nothing that throws any light on that woman."

Wallander closed the file containing all the documents relevant to the property.

"We must talk to the neighbors," he said. "The closest ones, at least. Do you know if Karl Eriksson was especially friendly with any of them?"

"If anybody, I suppose it would be the people in that pink house on the left just after you turn into the side road. There's an old milking stool standing outside it."

Wallander knew which house and milking stool Martinson was referring to. He also had a vague memory of someone there once buying one of his father's paintings. He couldn't remember if it had been one with or without a great grouse.

"There's an old lady there called Elin," said Martinson. "Elin Trulsson. She's been to visit Karl a few times—but she's also old. Maybe not quite as senile as he is, though."

Wallander stood up.

"Tomorrow," he said. "We'll talk to her tomorrow."

CHAPTER 11

Linda surprised Wallander by having dinner ready when he came back home. Although it was an ordinary weekday he was tempted to open a bottle of wine—but if he did Linda would only start stirring up trouble, so he didn't. Instead he told her about the return visit he and Martinson had made in Löderup.

"Did you find anything?"

"I now have an overall view of who owned the property over the past fifty years. But, of course, it's too early to say whether that knowledge will prove to be useful to us."

"I spoke to Stefan. He hadn't discovered any missing woman who might fit in the picture."

"I didn't expect he would."

They ate in silence. It was only when they came to the coffee that they resumed talking.

"You could have bought the house," she said. "You could have lived there until the day you died without knowing that there was a cemetery in your garden; lived there for the rest of your life without knowing that every summer you walked around in your bare feet on grass that was growing over a grave."

"I keep thinking about that hand," he said. "Something had caused it to come up to the surface. Obviously, if you have a tendency to believe in ghosts you might well think that the hand was sticking up on purpose in order to attract the attention of a visiting police officer."

Their conversation was interrupted by a call to Linda's cell phone. She answered, listened, then hung up.

"That was Stefan. I'm going to drive over to his place."

Wallander immediately felt that nagging feeling of jealousy. He made an unintentional grimace, which of course she noticed.

"What's the matter?"

"Nothing."

"I can see that there *is* something. You're pulling a face."

"That's just because something's got caught in my teeth."

"When will you learn that you can never get away with telling me lies?"

"I'm just a simple, jealous old father. That's all."

"Find yourself a woman. You know what I've said. If you don't find someone to fuck soon, you'll die."

"You know I don't like you using words like that."

"I think you need somebody to annoy you sometimes. Bye."

Linda left the room. Wallander thought for a few moments. Then he stood up, opened the bottle of wine, took out a glass and went into the living room. He dug out a record of Beethoven's last string quartet and sat down in his armchair. His thoughts started to wander as he listened to the music. The wine was making him dozy. He closed his eyes, and was soon half asleep.

He suddenly opened his eyes. He was wide awake again. The music was finished—the record had come to an end. A thought had struck him deep in his subconscious mind. That hand he had stumbled over. He had received an explanation from Nyberg that the forensic officer thought was plausible. Groundwater could rise and fall, the clay soil could sink down and hence force the undersoil up toward the surface. And so the hand had risen up to ground level. But why just the hand? Was that remark at the dinner table more significant than he had realized? Had that hand risen to the surface specifically in order to be observed?

He poured another glass of wine, then telephoned

Nyberg. It was always a bit dodgy calling him because he could object angrily to someone disturbing him. Wallander waited, listening to the phone ringing at the other end.

"Nyberg."

"It's Kurt. I hope I'm not disturbing you."

"Of course you're disturbing me, for Christ's sake. What do you want?"

"That hand sticking up out of the ground. The one I stumbled over. You said that the clay soil keeps shifting, gliding around, and that the groundwater level is changing constantly. But I still don't understand why that hand should emerge through the topsoil just now."

"Who said it happened just now? I didn't. It could have been lying there for many years."

"But surely somebody ought to have seen it in that case?"

"That's a problem for you to solve. Was that all?"

"Not really. Would it be possible for the hand to have been placed there on purpose? Specifically for it to be discovered? Did you notice if the ground there had been dug up recently?"

Nyberg was breathing heavily. Wallander was worried that he might burst into a fit of rage.

"That hand had moved there of its own accord," said Nyberg.

He hadn't become angry.

"It was exactly that I was wondering about," said Wallander. "Thank you for taking the trouble to respond."

He hung up and returned to his glass of wine.

Linda returned home shortly after midnight. By then he had already gone to bed and fallen asleep, after washing his glass and hiding away the empty bottle.

CHAPTER 12

At a quarter past ten the next day, October 29, Martinson and Wallander drove along the slushy roads to Löderup in order to speak to Elin Trulsson, and possibly other neighbors, in an attempt to find out more about who had been living in that house many years ago.

Earlier that morning they had attended a meeting, which had turned out to be very brief. Lisa Holgersson had insisted that no extra resources could be allocated to the investigation into the skeleton until the forensic report was completed.

"Winter," said Martinson. "I hate all this slush. I buy scratch cards and scrape away hopefully. I don't envisage masses of banknotes raining down over me: instead I see a house somewhere in Spain or on the Riviera."

"What would you do there?"

"Make long-pile rugs. Just think of all the slush and wet feet I'd avoid."

"You'd be bored stiff," said Wallander. "You'd make your damned rugs covered in motifs depicting snow-storms, and you'd long to be back here in this shitty weather."

They turned into the drive leading to the pink house a few hundred meters from Karl Eriksson's property. A middle-aged man was just about to clamber onto his tractor. He looked at them with a surprised look on his face. They all shook hands. The man introduced himself as Evert Trulsson, the owner of the neighboring farm. Wallander explained why they had come there.

"Who would have thought anything like that about Karl?" he said when Wallander had finished.

"Thought anything like what?"

"That he'd have a dead body buried in his garden."

Wallander glanced at Martinson and tried to understand the strange logic in what Evert Trulsson had said.

"Can you explain what you mean? Are you suggesting that he buried the body himself?"

"I've no idea. What do you know about your neighbors nowadays? In the old days you used to know more or less everything about the people you had around you. But now you haven't a clue about anything."

Wallander wondered if he had before him one of those

ultraconservative people who had no doubt that everything used to be better in the old days. He made up his mind not to be dragged into a pointless conversation.

"Elin Trulsson," he said. "Who's she?"

"She's my mother."

"We understand that she's been to visit Karl Eriksson in his care home."

"I have an old mum who cares about other people. I think she visits Karl because nobody else does."

"So they were friends, were they?"

"We were neighbors. That's not the same as being friends."

"But you weren't enemies," said Martinson.

"No. We were neighbors. Our farms had shared borders. We had shared responsibility for this street. We looked after our own business, we said hello and we helped each other out when it was necessary. But we didn't socialize."

"According to the information I have, the Erikssons came here in 1968. Thirty-four years ago. And they bought their property from somebody called Gustav Henander."

"I remember that. We were related to Henander. I think my dad was a half brother to someone called Henander, but Henander was an adopted child. I don't really know much about it. My mum might remember. You should ask her. My dad died ages ago."

They walked to the house.

"Gustav and Laura Henander had three children," said Martinson. "Two boys and a girl. But was there anybody else who used to live there? A woman, perhaps?"

"No. And we saw everybody who drove past our house. The Henanders lived on their own, and they never had any visitors."

They went into the warm kitchen, where two fat cats lay on a window ledge, eyeing them vigilantly. A middle-aged woman came into the room. It was Evert Trulsson's wife. She shook hands with them and said her name was Hanna. Wallander thought her hand was completely limp.

"There's coffee," said Evert Trulsson. "Sit down and I'll fetch my mum."

It was fifteen minutes before Evert Trulsson returned to the kitchen with his mother Elin. Wallander and Martinson had tried to converse with Hanna Trulsson, without making much progress. It occurred to Wallander that all he had learned during that quarter of an hour was that one of the cats was called Jeppe and the other one Florry.

Elin Trulsson was a very old woman. She had a furrowed face, and the wrinkles dug deep into her skin. It seemed to Wallander that she was very handsome—like an old tree trunk. This was not a new comparison as far as he was concerned. It had first occurred to him some time ago when he was looking at his father's face. There was a sort of beauty that only comes with age. A whole life engraved into facial wrinkles.

They shook hands. Unlike Hanna Trulsson, her mother-in-law gripped Wallander's hand firmly.

"I don't hear well," Elin Trulsson said. "I can't hear anything in my left ear; I can with my right, but only if people don't all talk at the same time."

"I've explained the situation to my mum," said Evert Trulsson.

Wallander leaned toward the old woman. Martinson had a notebook in his hand.

But Martinson's notebook remained blank. Elin Trulsson had absolutely nothing of significance to tell. Karl Eriksson and his wife had lived a life that evidently didn't conceal any secrets, nor did she have anything of interest to say about the Henanders. Wallander tried to take one more step back in time to Ludvig Hansson, who had sold the farm to Henander in 1949.

"I wasn't living here at that time," said Elin Trulsson. "I was working in Malmö in those days."

"How long had Ludvig Hansson owned the property?" Wallander asked.

Elin Trulsson looked questioningly at her son. He shook his head.

"I suppose they'd been living here for many generations," he said. "But that's no doubt information you could dig out."

Wallander could see that they weren't going to get

any further. He nodded to Martinson, they said thank you for the coffee, shook hands again, and left the house accompanied by Evert Trulsson. The sleet had turned into rain.

"It's a pity my dad isn't still alive," said Wallander. "He had an amazing memory. And he was also a bit of a local historian. But he never wrote anything down. He was better than most at telling the tales, though. If I hadn't been so thick I'd have recorded what he had to say on tape."

He was just about to get into his car when he realized that he had one more question to ask.

"Can you remember if anybody has gone missing in this area? During your time here or earlier? People tend to talk about things like that—missing persons in mysterious circumstances."

Evert Trulsson thought for a moment before answering.

"There was a teenage girl who disappeared from around here in the middle of the fifties. Nobody knows what happened to her—if she committed suicide or ran away or whatever. She was about fourteen or fifteen. Her name was Elin, just like my mum. But I don't know about anybody else."

Wallander and Martinson drove back to Ystad.

"That's it for now, then," said Wallander. "We don't lift a finger until the forensic medicine crowd in Lund have said what they have to say. Let's hope that despite everything it turns out to have been a natural death—

then all we would need to do is to try to identify the person. But if we fail, it won't be all that big a deal."

"Of course it was an unnatural death," said Martinson. "But apart from that I agree with you. We'll just wait."

They returned to Ystad and turned their attention to other business.

A few days later, on Friday, November 1, Skåne was subjected to a snowstorm. Traffic came to a standstill, and all police resources were concentrated on clearing up the situation that ensued. It stopped snowing the following afternoon, November 2. On Sunday it started raining. What was left of the snow was washed away.

The following Monday morning, November 4, Linda and Wallander walked together to the police station. They had barely entered reception when Martinson came storming down the corridor. He was carrying a bunch of papers in his hand.

Wallander could see straightaway that they came from the Center for Forensic Medicine in Lund.

CHAPTER 13

Stina Hurlén and her colleagues in Lund had done a good job. They still needed more time to investigate the woman whose skeleton had been found, but the information they could produce and confirm now was sufficient for Wallander and his colleagues to know what they were up against. In the first place, it really was a murder that had been committed. The woman had been killed. She had all the injuries typical of somebody who had been hanged. The injuries to the bones at the back of her neck were what had killed her. Wallander made the sardonic comment that it was usual for suicides to hang themselves, but not for them to go on to cut themselves down and bury themselves in their own or somebody else's garden.

They also received confirmation that Hurlén's guess about the woman being around fifty was in fact correct. That was her age when she died. The skeleton showed no signs of injuries caused by wear and tear: so the woman lying in the grave was not someone who had indulged in hard physical labor.

But it was the last item in the report that made Wallander and his colleagues feel they had received a significant piece of information they could work around—the handle that all police officers look for in a criminal investigation.

The woman had been lying in her grave for between fifty and seventy years. Exactly how the medics and various experts had reached that conclusion was beyond Wallander's comprehension. But he trusted it. The forensic experts were very rarely wrong.

Wallander took Martinson and Linda with him into his office, where they sat around his desk. Linda was not actually involved in the case, but she was following developments out of curiosity. And Wallander had learned to appreciate her spontaneous comments. Sometimes she came out with something that immediately proved to be important.

"The time," said Wallander when they had settled down. "What's the significance of that?"

"So she died at some point between 1930 and 1950," said Martinson. "That makes things both easier and more difficult. Easier because we now have a limited time to search through. More difficult because it's so long ago."

Wallander smiled. "That was neatly put," he said. "Different. 'We have a limited time to search through.' Searching through time. Maybe you ought to become a poet in another existence."

He leaned forward, suddenly inspired by a burst of energy. Now they had something to hold onto. The handle was in place.

"We'll have to start rummaging around," he said. "We'll have to work our way through piles of dusty papers. Whatever happened took place when we'd barely been born—least of all Linda. But I'm beginning to be very interested in who that woman was, and what exactly happened."

"I've just been doing some mental arithmetic," said Linda. "If we assume she was murdered in 1940, just to pick a point in time between the two limits mentioned, and if we take it that the murderer was an adult—let's say about thirty or so—that means we're looking for somebody who's about ninety years old. A ninety-year-old murderer. And he could even be over a hundred. Which presumably means he's been dead for ages."

"Correct," said Wallander. "But we don't call it a day simply because a murderer is presumably dead. What we start by doing is finding out who this woman was. Then we might hear from relatives, perhaps even children, who will be relieved if they find out what happened."

"In other words, we become sort of archaeological police officers," said Martinson. "It'll be interesting to hear what degree of priority Lisa gives it."

The answer to that, as Wallander had expected, was none at all. Lisa Holgersson recognized, of course, that the discovery of the skeleton needed to be investigated, but she couldn't grant them any extra resources since there were so many other cases that were waiting urgently to be concluded.

"I have the National Police Board breathing down my neck, with all the boxes we have to tick and paperwork to send them," she sighed. "We have to demonstrate that we're being successful with our inquiries. We can no longer get away with reporting shelved investigations as solved."

Both Martinson and Wallander gave a start. Wallander suspected that Lisa Holgersson might have said too much. Or maybe she just wanted to share her frustration.

"Is that really possible?" asked Wallander cautiously.

"Everything is possible. I'm just waiting for the day when the National Audit Office discovers that we've been recording shelved investigations as solved."

"We'll be the ones who suffer," said Wallander. "We'll be the ones the general public blame."

"No," said Martinson. "People aren't that stupid. They see that there are fewer and fewer of us. They recognize that it's not us who are the problem."

Lisa Holgersson stood up. The meeting was closed. She

had no desire to continue an unpleasant conversation about any sleight of hand concerning unsolved—and yet solved—criminal cases.

Martinson and Wallander headed toward one of the conference rooms. They bumped into Linda in the corridor. She was on her way out to one of the patrol cars.

"How did it go?"

"As expected," said Wallander. "We have too much to do, and so we should do as little as we can."

"That was an unjust comment," said Martinson.

"Of course it was unjust. Who said that police work had anything to do with justice?"

Linda shook her head and left.

"I didn't understand that last comment you made," said Martinson.

"Neither did I," said Wallander cheerfully. "But it does no harm to give the younger generation something to think about."

They sat down at the table. Martinson contacted Stefan Lindman on the intercom; he arrived after a few minutes, carrying a file.

"Missing persons," said Wallander. "Nothing fascinates the public at large like people who go up in smoke. People who go out to buy a bottle of milk and never come back. Or visit a girlfriend and are never seen again. Young women who go missing never fail to stimulate the general public's imagination. I still remember a girl called Ulla who disappeared after a dance in Sundbyberg sometime in the fifties. She was never seen again. I can still conjure up her face whenever I think about her."

"There are some statistics," said Stefan Lindman. "They're pretty reliable, given that they come from the police . . . Most people reported as missing usually turn up again very soon—after just a couple of days, or maybe a week. Only a few never return."

He opened the file.

"I've dug down into the past," he said. "In order to cover the time the medics think we should be looking at, I've fished out information relevant to the period 1935 to 1955. Our registers—even the old ones and those dealing with unsolved investigations at various points in time—are pretty detailed. I think I've produced quite a good picture of the overall situation, and the missing women who might be of interest."

Wallander leaned forward over the table.

"So what have you to tell us?"

"Nothing."

"Nothing?"

Stefan Lindman nodded.

"Your ears are not deceiving you. During the period of time in question there wasn't a single woman in the appropriate age range who was reported as missing in this area. Nor was there anybody in Malmö. I thought I'd found a woman who might be the one we were after—a forty-nine-year-old from Svedala who went missing in December 1942. But she turned up again a few years later.

She had left her husband and gone off with a soldier from Stockholm who had been stationed here. But she grew tired of him, the passion cooled down, and she came back home. There's nothing at all apart from her."

They thought over what Stefan Lindman had said, in silence.

"So nobody is reported missing," said Martinson after a while. "But a woman was buried in a garden. She had been murdered. Somebody must have missed her."

"She could have come from somewhere else," said Lindman. "A list of all the women of the appropriate age in Sweden who have gone missing during those years would produce a quite different result, naturally. Besides, there was a war on, and a lot of people were constantly on the move. Including refugees, who were not always registered officially, as they ought to have been."

Wallander followed a different line of thought.

"This is how I see it," he said. "We don't know who the woman is—but we do know where she was buried. Somebody picked up a spade and buried her. There's no reason to believe that was anybody but the man who killed her. Or the woman—that's not impossible of course. That ought to be our starting point. Who held the spade? Why was the body buried in Karl Eriksson's garden?"

"Not Karl Eriksson's garden," said Martinson. "Ludvig Hansson's garden."

Wallander nodded.

"That's where we must start," he said. "With Ludwig Hansson and his family who owned the place in those days. All those who were alive then are now dead. Apart from those who were children at the time. That's where we should begin: with Ludvig Hansson's children."

"Shall I carry on searching?" wondered Lindman. "With the rest of Sweden? All missing women between 1935 and 1955?"

"Yes," said Wallander. "That woman must have been reported missing somewhere or other. She must be there somewhere."

CHAPTER 14

It took Wallander three days to trace Ludvig Hansson's only child who was still in the land of the living. Meanwhile, Stefan Lindman had begun to make a list of Swedish women who had gone missing during the years in question, and had found a couple who at least were about the right age. But what made him and his colleagues doubtful was that both women came from the north of Sweden: one of them lived in Timrå just outside Sundsvall when she disappeared, and the other, Maria Teresa Arbåge, had been living in Luleå when she was reported missing.

Martinson had been scouring the land register and was able to confirm that the farm Ludvig Hansson had sold had been in his family since the middle of the nineteenth century. The first Hansson had actually been called Hansen, and came from close to the Småland border, some way north of Ystad. On several occasions Wallander and Martinson discussed why the family property had suddenly been sold. Could that be linked with a motive that could throw light on the woman in the garden?

Linda had also come up with a suggestion that Wallander had recognized, somewhat reluctantly, was an excellent one. She proposed trying to track down old aerial photographs of the property, older than the one hanging on the wall of the house in Löderup. Had the garden undergone change? If so, when? And what had happened to the wing that had originally been attached to the house, but now no longer existed?

Wallander had delved into population registers and in the end discovered the only one of Ludvig Hansson's four children who was still alive. It was a woman by the name of Kristina, who was born in 1937. Wallander established that she was an afterthought, born to Ludvig and his wife Alma several years after the rest of her siblings. Kristina had eventually married and changed her surname to Fredberg. She now lived in Malmö, and Wallander felt a pang of excitement when he picked up the telephone and rang her.

It was a young woman who answered. He said his name and informed her that he was a police officer, and asked to speak to Kristina. The woman asked him to wait.

Kristina Fredberg had a friendly voice. Wallander

explained the situation, and said he needed to talk to her in connection with the investigation into the discovery that had been made in the garden.

"I've read about it in the newspaper," she said. "I find it hard to believe that such a thing could happen in the garden where I played as a child. Have you no idea at all whose body it is?"

"No."

"I hardly think I have anything of significance to tell you."

"I need to create a picture. An overall picture."

"You're welcome to come around whenever you like," she said. "I have all the time in the world. I'm a widow. My husband died two years ago. He had cancer. It went quickly."

"Was it your daughter who answered the phone?"

"Lena. She's my youngest. The entry code number is 1225."

They agreed that Wallander would drive to central Malmö to meet her that same day. Without really knowing why, he telephoned Linda and asked her if she would like to accompany him. She had the day off after working two successive nights, and he woke her up. But, unlike her father, she seldom became angry when her beauty sleep was interrupted. They agreed that he would collect her an hour later, at eleven o'clock.

It was wet and windy when they drove out to Malmö. Wallander listened to a cassette recording of *La bohème*.

As Linda was not especially keen on opera he had turned the volume down. When they came to Svedala, Wallander switched the music off altogether.

"Nobelvägen," he said. "She lives right in the center."

"Have we time to stay on for a bit afterward?" asked Linda. "I want to do some shopping. It's ages since I've been to any decent shops."

"What kind of shopping?"

"Clothes. I want to buy a sweater. As consolation."

"Consolation for what?"

"For feeling rather lonely."

"How are things with you and Stefan?"

"It's going well. But one can feel lonely at times, even so."

Wallander said nothing. He knew all too well what Linda was talking about.

He parked the car at Triangeln. The wind was bitter while they were finding their way to the house. Wallander had written the entry code number on the back of his hand.

Kristina Fredberg's apartment was on the top floor. There was no elevator. Wallander was panting heavily by the time they reached the top of the stairs. Linda stared sternly at him.

"You'll have a heart attack if you don't start exercising soon."

"There's nothing wrong with my heart. I've been on an exercise bike with wires attached to my body, and the result was good. And my average blood pressure is 135 over 80. That's also good. And my blood lipids are as they should be. Well, almost. I have my diabetes under control. In addition to all that I have my prostate checked once a year. Will that do, or would you like all that information in writing?"

"You're mad," said Linda. "But quite funny. Ring the doorbell now."

Kristina Fredberg looked distinctly youthful. Wallander found it difficult to believe that she was sixty-five years old. He'd have guessed just over fifty if he hadn't known.

She invited them into her living room. A tray with coffee and biscuits was on the table. They had just sat down when a woman of Linda's age came in through the door. She introduced herself as Lena. Wallander couldn't remember when he had last seen such a beautiful woman. She looked like her mother, and spoke like her, with the same voice and a smile that gave Wallander a forbidden urge to touch her.

"Do you mind if I sit in and listen?" she asked. "From pure curiosity."

"Not at all," said Wallander.

She sat down on the sofa next to her mother. Wallander couldn't resist looking at her legs. Then he noticed that Linda was frowning at him. Why did I ask her to come with me? he wondered. To give her even more reason to criticize me?

Kristina Fredberg served coffee. Wallander took out

his notebook and pencil. But needless to say, he had forgotten his glasses. He put the notebook back into his pocket.

"You were born in 1937," he said. "You were the youngest of four siblings."

"I was an afterthought, yes. I don't think I was really wanted. More of a mistake."

"Why do you think that?"

"It's the sort of thing children sense. But nobody ever said anything."

"And you grew up there at the house in Löderup?"

"Yes and no. Until 1942, in November, we lived there all the year round. Then Mum and I and my brothers and sister moved to Malmö for a few years."

"Why?"

Wallander noticed that she hesitated very slightly before answering.

"My mother and father had fallen out. But they didn't divorce. I don't know what happened. We lived in a flat in Limhamn for a few years. Then, in the spring of 1945, we moved back to Löderup. They had become reconciled. When she was older, I tried to ask my mother why they had fallen out, but she didn't want to talk about it. I asked my siblings as well. We don't think anything special happened. The marriage just suddenly fell apart. My mother moved out and took her children with her. But then they became friends again and remained together until she died. I remember my parents as people who liked one another. What happened when I was a little girl during the war is now just a vague memory. An unpleasant memory."

"So your father remained living at the farm in Löderup during those years, did he?"

"He had animals that needed looking after. My elder brother said that he employed two farmhands. One of them came from Denmark, as a refugee. But nobody knows any details. My father wasn't very talkative."

Wallander thought for a moment. There was an obvious question to ask.

"So he hadn't met another woman?"

"No."

"How can you be so sure?"

"I just know."

"Can you explain in a little more detail?"

"My mother would never have moved back to the house if my father had had a lover. And it wouldn't have been possible to keep it secret."

"My experience is that you can have secrets no matter where you live."

Wallander noticed that Linda raised her eyebrows with interest.

"No doubt you can. But not from my mother. Her intuition was something I've never come across in any other person."

"Apart from me," said her daughter Lena.

"That's right. You've inherited it from your grand-mother. Nobody can hide the truth from you either."

Kristina Fredberg sounded convincing. Wallander was sure that she was not intentionally trying to conceal anything that could be of value to the police. But could she really be so certain about what her father had been doing when he lived alone at the farm for those three years during the war?

"Those farmhands," he said. "One came from Den-mark, did he? What was his name?"

"Jörgen. I remember that. But he's dead. He had some illness or other—something to do with his kidneys, I believe. He died in the fifties."

"But there was a second one?"

"So my brother Ernst maintained. I never heard a name."

"Perhaps there are pictures? Or records of wage payments?"

"I think my father paid cash in hand. And I've never seen any photographs."

Wallander served himself some more coffee.

"Could the other farmhand have been a woman?" asked Linda suddenly.

As usual Wallander was annoyed when he felt that she was trespassing on his territory. She was welcome to be present and learn a thing or two, but she should avoid taking any initiatives without consulting him first.

"No," said Kristina Fredberg. "There were no female farmhands in those days. Housekeepers, perhaps; but not farmhands. I'm absolutely convinced that my father did not have an affair with any other woman. I don't know who it is lying buried in the garden. The very thought makes me shudder. But I'm sure my father had nothing to do with what happened. Even if he lived there at the time."

"Why are you so sure? Please forgive me for asking the question."

"My father was a friendly, peaceful man. He never touched another person. I can't remember him ever smacking one of my brothers. He simply lacked the ability to get angry. Surely you must have a streak of uncontrolled fury in order to kill another human being? I think so in any case."

For now, Wallander had only one question left to ask.

"Your brothers and sister are dead—but is there anybody else you think I ought to talk to? Somebody who might have some memory of this?"

"It's all so long ago. Everybody from my parents' generation died ages ago. As you say, my brothers and sister are also dead. I've no idea who else might be able to help you."

Wallander stood up. He shook hands with the two women. Then he and Linda left the apartment.

When they came out into the street below, she stood in front of him.

"I don't want a dad who starts drooling at the sight of a pretty young girl who is younger than I am."

Wallander reacted vehemently.

"What are you trying to suggest? I didn't drool. I thought she was pretty, yes. But don't try to tell me that I did anything improper. If you do, you can take the train back to Ystad. And you can move out of my apartment and live somewhere else."

Wallander strode off. She didn't catch up with him until he reached the car. She stood in front of him again.

"I'm sorry. I didn't mean to offend you."

"I don't want you to tell me how to behave. I don't want you forcing me to be somebody I'm not."

"I've said I'm sorry."

"I heard you."

Linda wanted to say something else, but Wallander held up his hand. That was enough. There was no need to say any more.

They drove back to Ystad. They didn't start talking again until after they had passed Svaneholm. Linda agreed with him that, despite everything, something must have happened during the years when Ludvig Hansson was living alone on his farm.

Wallander tried hard to envisage what it might have been, but he could see nothing. Only that hand sticking up out of the ground.

The wind was even stronger now. It struck him that winter was just around the corner.

CHAPTER 15

The following day, Friday, November 8, Wallander woke up early. He was sweaty. He tried to remember what he had been dreaming about—it was something to do with Linda, perhaps a rerun of the confrontation they had had the previous day. But his memory was empty. The dream had closed all the doors surrounding it.

It was ten minutes to five. He lay there in the darkness. The rain was pounding against his bedroom window. He tried to go back to sleep, but failed. After tossing and turning until six o'clock, he got up. He paused outside Linda's door: she was asleep, snoring softly.

He made some coffee and sat down in the kitchen. The rain was coming and going. Without really thinking about it, he decided to begin his working day by making another visit to the property where they had found the skeleton. He had no idea what he hoped to gain by doing so, but he often returned to crime scenes, not least to reassess his first impressions.

He left Ystad half an hour later, and when he arrived at the house in Löderup it wasn't yet light. The police tape was still in place, cordoning off the scene. He walked slowly around the house and garden. All the time he was looking out for something he hadn't noticed before. He had no idea what that might be. Something that didn't fit in, something that stood out. At the same time he tried to imagine a possible sequence of events.

Once upon a time a woman lived here, but never left the place. Yet somebody must have wondered what had happened to her. And it is obvious that nobody has ever been here, looking for her. Nobody has suspected anything that has led to the police investigating this property.

He paused next to the grave, which was now covered by a dirty tarpaulin.

Why was the body buried just here? The garden is large. Somebody must have thought about alternatives, and made a decision. Here, just here, not anywhere else.

Wallander started walking again, but stored away in his memory the questions he had formulated. He could hear a tractor in the background. A lone red kite was soaring up above, then swooped down onto one of the fields that surrounded the property. He went back to the grave, and looked around. He suddenly noticed a place next to some currant bushes. At first he didn't know what had attracted his attention: it was something to do with the relationship of the bushes to one another. A characteristic of the garden as a whole was symmetry: everything was planted in a way that created a pattern. Even though the garden was neglected and very overgrown, he could still see all those patterns. And there was something about the currant bushes that didn't fit in.

The bushes were an exception that went against the rule that held sway in the garden as a whole.

After a few minutes the penny dropped. It wasn't a pattern that had been broken: it was a pattern that was no longer there. Several currant bushes were in the wrong place, in this garden that was based on a pattern of straight lines.

He went back and examined the area more closely. There was no doubt about it, some of the bushes were in the wrong place. But as far as he could see the bushes had not been planted at different times—they all seemed to be the same age.

He thought for a while. The only explanation he could think of was that at some point the bushes had been dug up, and then replanted by somebody with no sense of the garden's symmetry.

But then it occurred to him that there might be another explanation. Whoever dug up the bushes and then replanted them might have been in a hurry.

It was starting to get light now. It was almost eight o'clock. He sat down on one of the moss-covered stone chairs and continued to study the currant bushes. Was he just imagining it all, despite everything?

After another quarter of an hour he was certain. The haphazard planting of the currant bushes told a story. About somebody who was either careless, or had been in a hurry. Or of course the person might come into both categories.

He took out his cell phone and rang Nyberg, who had just arrived at the police station.

"I'm sorry I rang you so late the other day," said Wallander.

"If you were really sorry you'd have stopped ages ago ringing me at all hours of the day and night. You've frequently rung me at four or five in the morning without having any questions that couldn't have waited until a decent time of day. I don't recall you apologizing any of those times."

"Perhaps I've become a better person."

"Don't talk shit! What do you want?"

Wallander told him where he was, and about his feeling that something was wrong. Nyberg was a person who would understand the significance of currant bushes planted in the wrong place.

"I'll come out there," said Nyberg when Wallander had finished. "But I'll be on my own. Do you have a spade in your car?"

"No. But no doubt there'll be one in the shed some-where."

"That's not what I meant. I have my own spade. I just wanted to make sure that you wouldn't start rooting around yourself before I got there."

"I'll do nothing at all until you arrive."

They hung up. Wallander sat in his car, as he was feeling cold. He listened somewhat absentmindedly to the car radio. Somebody was going on about a new infectious disease that they suspected was spread by common ticks.

He switched off the radio and waited.

Nineteen minutes later Nyberg turned into the yard. He was wearing Wellington boots, overalls and a strange old hunting hat pulled down over his ears. He took a spade out of the trunk.

"I suppose we can be pleased that you didn't stumble over that hand after the frost had made it impossible to dig in the soil."

"Surely the ground doesn't get frozen before Christmas in these parts? If it ever does."

Nyberg mumbled something inaudible in response. They went to the spot in question at the back of the house. Wallander could see that Nyberg had understood the significance of his observations about the currant bushes without needing further explanation. Nyberg tested the ground with the edge of his spade, as if he were looking for something.

"The soil is pretty tightly packed," he said. "Which

suggests that it's been a long time since anybody was digging here. The roots from the bushes bind the soil together."

He started digging. Wallander stood to one side, watching. After only a few minutes, Nyberg stopped digging and pointed down at the soil. He picked up something that looked like a stone and handed it to Wallander.

It was a tooth. A human tooth.

CHAPTER 16

Two days later, the whole of Karl Eriksson's garden had been dug up. At the spot where Nyberg had picked up the tooth and handed it to Wallander, they had found a skeleton that Stina Hurlén and other forensic medicine experts had concluded was the remains of a man. He was also in his fifties at the time of death, and had also been lying in that grave for a long time. But there was an injury to his skull that suggested a blow from a heavy instrument.

There had naturally been an outburst of excitement when news of the discovery of a second skeleton reached the mass media. Large black headlines proclaimed "THE GARDEN OF DEATH" or "DEATH IN THE CURRANT BUSHES."

Lisa Holgersson could no longer limit the allocation of resources. Wallander was put in charge of the case along with a female prosecutor, who had just returned from study leave during which she had undergone further training. She told Wallander to take his time, and to be thorough in all aspects of the investigation. Until the identity of those who had been buried in the garden had been established, there was very little that could be done with regard to finding a culprit.

Stefan Lindman continued to search through registers and old cases which might possibly give them a clue they could follow up. At first they had been looking for one woman. Now it was two missing persons. The general public came up with various tips—shadows of people who had disappeared mysteriously many years ago. Wallander allocated another police officer to assist Lindman in making a rough preliminary assessment of all the tips they received.

After two weeks, they still hadn't got anywhere when it came to identifying the two dead bodies. Wallander gathered together all his assistants one Thursday afternoon in the large conference room, asked everybody to switch off their cell phones, and gave a thorough account of what had happened so far. They went back to the start, reassessed the forensic and medical reports, and listened to what Wallander described as a brilliant presentation by Stefan Lindman. After four hours, when everything had been discussed ad nauseam, Wallander adjourned the meeting briefly and aired the room, then reassembled everybody for a summary.

He used five words to say what they all knew already. *We're still at square one.*

They had two skeletons, the remains of two middle-aged people who had been murdered. But they had no identities, and didn't even have any potentially rewarding leads to follow up.

"The past has closed all doors behind it," said Wallander when the formal summary was complete and they were talking more freely about what had happened.

There was no need to allocate new duties—they were already following the only routes open to them. They would make no progress until they discovered new information about who these two people could have been.

During the two weeks that had passed Wallander and Martinson had tried, with increasing levels of impatience, to find people who could remember a little more about the years during the war when Ludvig Hansson had lived alone on the farm. But they were all dead. Wallander had a recurrent, creepy feeling that what he really ought to be doing was to set up interrogations with all the gravestones in nearby cemeteries. That was where all conceivable witnesses, and any others who might have been involved, were to be found now. There might even be a murderer lying there, with all the answers Wallander and his colleagues were looking for.

Martinson shared his superior's feelings with regard to the seemingly hopeless search for some living person who could be of assistance to them. But they did not give up, of course. They followed their routines, kept sifting through various archives and old criminal investigations—looking for people who might still be alive and could possibly have something of interest to tell them.

One evening when Wallander returned home with a headache, Linda sat down opposite him at the kitchen table and asked how things were going.

"We're not giving up," he said. "We never give up."

She asked no more questions. She knew her father.

He had said all he had to say.

CHAPTER 17

The next day, November 29, it was snowing heavily over Skåne. A storm was blowing in from the west, and flights were disrupted at Sturup airport for several hours. Lots of cars skidded off the road between Malmö and Ystad. But after a few hours, the strong wind suddenly dropped, it became warmer, and it began to rain.

Wallander stood at his window in the police station, gazing out over the road and noting how the snow suddenly became rain. The telephone rang. As usual he gave a start. He answered it.

"It's Simon," said a voice.

"Simon?"

"Simon Larsson. Once upon a time we used to be colleagues."

Wallander thought at first that he had misunderstood what had been said. Simon Larsson had been a police officer when Wallander had come to Ystad from Malmö. That was a long time ago. Simon Larsson had been old even then. Two years after Wallander's arrival in Ystad Larsson had retired and been formally thanked at a party hosted by the then chief of police. As far as Wallander was aware, Simon Larsson had never set foot inside the police station since then. He had severed all contact. Wallander had heard a rumor that Larsson had an apple orchard just north of Simrishamn to which he devoted all his time.

He was surprised to hear that Simon Larsson was evidently still alive. He did the mental arithmetic and concluded that Larsson must now be at least eighty-five.

"I remember who you are," said Wallander. "But I must say that this call has come as a surprise."

"No doubt you thought I was dead. I sometimes think I am myself."

Wallander said nothing.

"I've read about the two people you found," said Larsson. "I might have something useful to say about it."

"What do you mean?"

"What I say. If you come around to my place, then maybe—but only maybe—I might have something useful to tell you." Simon Larsson spoke in a clear and lucid voice.

Wallander made a note of his address. It was a care

home for the elderly just outside Tomelilla. Wallander promised to visit him right away. He stopped in at Martinson's office but it was empty—his cell phone was lying on his desk. Wallander shrugged and decided to drive out to Tomelilla on his own.

Simon Larsson seemed to be in a fragile state. He had a wrinkled face and a hearing aid. He opened the door and Wallander entered a pensioner's apartment that was frightening in its dreariness. It seemed to Wallander that he was entering the hallway of death. The apartment comprised two rooms. Through a half-open door Wallander could see an old woman lying on top of a bed, resting. Hands shaking, Simon Larsson served up coffee. Wallander felt ill at ease. It was as if he were looking at himself at some time in the future. He didn't like what he saw. He sat down in a worn armchair. A cat immediately jumped up onto his knee. Wallander let it stay there. He preferred dogs, but he had nothing against cats that occasionally expressed an interest in him.

Simon Larsson sat down on a Windsor chair opposite him.

"I don't hear well, but I see well. I suppose it's a hangover from all my years as a police officer—wanting to see the people I'm talking to."

"I have the same problem," said Wallander. "Or custom, perhaps I ought to say. What was it you wanted to tell me?"

Simon Larsson took a deep breath, as if he needed to brace himself for what was about to come.

"I was born in August 1917," he said. "It was a warm summer, the year before the war ended. In 1937 I started working for the public prosecution service in Lund, and I came to Ystad in the sixties, after the police force had been nationalized. But what I wanted to tell you about, which might be of significance, happened during the forties. I worked for a few years then here in Tomelilla. They weren't so strict about borderlines in those days— sometimes we helped out in Ystad and sometimes they came to assist us here. Anyway, at some time during the war a horse and an old caravan were found on the road not far from Löderup."

"A horse? And a caravan? I don't really understand."

"You will if you stop interrupting me. It was in the autumn. Somebody rang us here in Tomelilla. Some bloke or other from Löderup. He ought to have tele-phoned Ystad, but instead he phoned the chief inspec-tor's office here in Tomelilla. He wanted to report that he had found a horse pulling a caravan along a road, without anybody inside or in the driver's seat. I was the only person around that morning. As I was learning to drive, I didn't bother ringing Ystad but instead took the car and drove to Löderup. Sure enough, there was a horse and caravan there, but no people. It was obvious from the inside of the caravan that gypsies lived in it.

Nowadays we're supposed to call them *travelers*, which makes them sound much more respectable. Anyway, they had vanished. It was all very odd. The horse and caravan had simply turned up there as dawn broke. Seven days earlier they had been seen in Kåseberga—a man and a woman in their fifties. He sharpened scissors and knives, they were friendly and reliable—but then they suddenly vanished."

"Were they ever found?"

"Not as far as I know. I thought this information might be of some use to you."

"Absolutely. What you say is very interesting. But it's odd that nobody reported them missing—if they had done they would have been in our register."

"I don't really know what happened. Somebody looked after the horse, and I suppose the caravan just rotted away. I suspect the fact is that nobody cared much about *travelers*. I recall asking about what had happened, a year or so later, but nobody knew anything. There was an awful lot of prejudice in those days. But perhaps there is now as well?"

"Can you remember anything else?"

"It was such a long time ago. I'm just glad I can remember what I've told you."

"Can you say what year it was?"

"No. But there was a fair bit about it in the newspapers at the time. It must be possible to find those articles."

Wallander felt the urge to act immediately. He drained his cup of coffee and stood up.

"Many thanks for getting in touch. This could well turn out to be important. I'll get back to you."

"Don't leave it too long," said Larsson. "I'm an old man. I could die at any time."

Wallander left Tomelilla. He drove fast. For the first time during this investigation, he had the feeling that they were about to make a breakthrough.

CHAPTER 18

It took Martinson four hours to find microfilm versions of *Ystads Allehanda* that contained articles about the mysterious horse and caravan. A few hours later he came to the police station with lots of copies of the microfilm pages. Together with Stefan Lindman, Wallander and Martinson sat down in the conference room.

"The fifth of December 1944," said Martinson. "That's when it begins. The headline over the first report of the incident in *Ystads Allehanda* is 'THE FLYING DUTCHMAN ON THE COUNTRY ROAD.'"

They spent the next hour reading through everything that Martinson had collected. Wallander noted that the two people who had lived in the caravan were called Richard and Irina Pettersson. There was even a blurred picture of them—a copy of a framed photograph hanging inside the caravan.

"Simon Larsson has a good memory," said Wallander when they had finished reading the articles. "We can be grateful for that. We might have caught on to this pair sooner or later, but you never know. The question is, of course: can these two be the people we are looking for?"

"They are the right age," said Lindman. "And the place fits in. The question is: what happened?"

"The records," said Wallander. "We need to dig out all the information we can find about them. If there really were such a thing as a time machine, now is when we could make use of it."

"Perhaps Nyberg has one," suggested Lindman.

Wallander and Martinson burst out laughing. Wallander stood up and walked over to the window. Martinson continued laughing in the background, and Lindman sneezed.

"Let's concentrate on this for the next few days," said Wallander. "We shouldn't abandon all the other leads, but we'll let them rest. Let them mature, as you might say. But something tells me this one is right. There are too many things that fit in for these not to be the two people we're looking for."

"Everybody in the newspapers speaks well of them," said Martinson. "But somewhere between the lines you get the feeling that people didn't care all that much about what happened to them. It's the mystery that captured everybody's attention. You get the impression that we should feel most sorry for the horse, pulling around an empty caravan. Just imagine what would have been said and written if it had been two old local farmers who had disappeared."

"You're right," said Wallander. "But until we know just who exactly those two people were, we can't exclude the possibility that they are somehow involved in the murder. I'll ring the prosecutor and tell her about this. OK, let's get going."

They agreed who would do what in their efforts to get a more detailed picture of Richard and Irina Pettersson who had gone missing sixty years ago. Wallander went to his office to ring the prosecutor and report on the new development, and was given the green light to go ahead as they had planned. Then he sat down and read through the newspaper articles one more time

When he had finished, he still felt strongly about it. He really did think they were finally on the right track.

CHAPTER 19

They carried on working hard until December 2. The weather in Skåne continued to be bad. Nonstop wind and rain. Wallander spent most of his time on the telephone or at the computer, which now, at last, after many years of trying, he had finally learned how to use. On the morning of December 2 he had tracked down one of Richard and Irina Pettersson's grandchildren. Her name was Katja Blomberg and she lived in Malmö. When he rang her it was a man who answered. Katja Blomberg was not at home, but Wallander left his telephone number and said it was urgent. He did not spell out any details.

He was still waiting for her to call back when he was contacted by reception.

"You have a visitor," said a receptionist whose voice he did not recognize.

"Who is it?"

"She says her name's Katja Blomberg."

Wallander held his breath.

"I'm coming."

He went out to the reception desk. Katja Blomberg was in her forties, heavily made up, and wore a short skirt and high-heeled boots. A few traffic police officers glanced enviously at Wallander as they passed. He shook hands with her. Her grip was strong.

"I thought I might just as well come here."

"That was kind of you."

"Of course it was kind of me. I could have just said bollocks, couldn't I? What is it you want?"

Wallander led her to his office. On the way he glanced in at Martinson's office: it was empty, as usual. Katja Blomberg sat down on the visitor chair and took out a packet of cigarettes.

"I'd rather you didn't," said Wallander.

"Do you want to talk to me or don't you?"

"I do, yes."

"Then I shall smoke. Just to put you in the picture."

Wallander felt that he didn't have the strength to argue with her. And in any case, cigarette smoke didn't irritate him all that much. He stood up to look for something that could serve as an ashtray.

"You needn't bother. I have an ashtray with me."

She placed a small metal beaker on the edge of the desk and lit her cigarette.

"It wasn't me," she said.

Wallander frowned. "I beg your pardon?"

"You heard what I said. I said it wasn't me."

Wallander raised an eyebrow. He realized she must be referring to something he knew nothing about.

"Who was it then?"

"I don't know."

Wallander reached for a notepad and a pencil.

"Just a few formalities," he said.

"620202-0445."

It was clear that Katja Blomberg had been in police custody before. He noted down her address, then excused himself and left the room. Martinson still wasn't in his office, but Wallander managed to contact Stefan Lindman and passed on the information.

"I want to know what we have on this woman."

"Now?"

"Now."

He explained briefly. Lindman understood. Wallander returned to his own office. It was heavy with tobacco smoke. Katja Blomberg smoked cigarettes without filters. He opened the window.

"It wasn't me," she said again.

"We'll come to that later," said Wallander. "Just now there's something else I want to talk to you about."

He could see that she was immediately on her guard.

"What?"

"I want to talk to you about your maternal grandmother and grandfather. Richard and Irina Pettersson."

"What the hell have they got to do with it?"

She stubbed out her cigarette and immediately lit a new one. Wallander noted that she had an expensive lighter.

"For various reasons I want to know what happened that time when they disappeared. You weren't born then. You were born twenty years later. But you must have heard about it."

She stared at him as if he was not quite right in the head.

"Have you got in touch with me to talk about that?"

"Not only that."

"But it was a hundred years ago."

"Not quite. Only a little short of sixty."

She looked him straight in the eye.

"I want some coffee."

"By all means. Milk and sugar?"

"Not milk. Cream and sugar."

"We don't have any cream. You can have milk. And sugar."

Wallander fetched some coffee. As there was something wrong with the machine it was nearly ten minutes before he returned. The room was empty. He cursed aloud. When he went back into the corridor he saw her approaching from the toilet.

"Did you think I'd escaped?"

"You've not been charged or arrested, so you can't escape."

They drank the coffee. Wallander waited. He wondered what it was she thought he wanted to talk to her about.

"Richard and Irina," he said again. "What can you tell me about them?"

Before she had time to reply the telephone rang. It was Stefan Lindman.

"That went quickly. Shall I tell you over the phone?"

"Yes, do."

"Katja Blomberg has been found guilty twice of assault. She's done time in Hinseberg. She also robbed a bank with a man she was married to for a few years. Now she's apparently one of several suspects in connection with a robbery from a grocer's shop in Limhamn. Shall I go on?"

"Not for the moment."

"How's it going?"

"We can talk about that later."

Wallander hung up and looked at Katja Blomberg, who was studying her nails: they were painted bright red, the shade varying from finger to finger.

"Your grandfather and your grandmother," he said. "Somebody must have told you about them. Not least your parents. Your mother. Is she still alive?"

"She died twenty years ago."

"Your father?"

She looked up from her nails.

"The last I heard of him was when I was six or seven years old. He was in jail for fraud. I've never been in touch with him. Nor him with me. I don't know if he's still alive. As far as I'm concerned I don't mind if he's dead. If you understand what I mean."

"I understand what you mean."

"Do you?"

"This will be over more quickly if you let me ask the questions. Surely your mother must have told you something about your grandparents?"

"There wasn't much to say."

"But they disappeared. Without trace. Isn't that something to talk about?"

"But good Lord! They came back again!"

Wallander stared at her.

"What do you mean by that?"

"What do you think I mean?"

"I want to know what you mean!"

"They came back. They left the caravan during the night, took some essentials with them, and disappeared. I think they lived on a farm up in Småland for a few years. Then when everything had quietened down they came back, changed their names, altered their hairstyles, and nobody asked any questions about the thefts anymore."

"Thefts?"

"Don't you know anything?"

"The reason you're here is so that you can explain it to me."

"They had burgled a farmer near here. But then they got cold feet. They took whatever they could carry, pretended to have disappeared, and kept out of the way. I think Richard called himself Arvid and Irina called herself Helena. I only saw them a few times. But I liked them. Grandad died at the beginning of the seventies, and Grandma a few years later. They're buried in the cemetery at Hässleholm. But not under their real names."

Wallander said nothing. He didn't doubt for a moment that what he had just heard was true. Every single word.

The abandoned horse and caravan in October 1942 had been a red herring. It had remained a red herring for sixty years.

There was disappointment, but at the same time relief in the knowledge that they hadn't wasted a lot of energy unnecessarily.

"Why are you asking about all this?"

"An investigation that has to be concluded. Two skeletons have been discovered in somebody's garden. Perhaps you've read about it in the newspapers? I'll leave the business of the grocer's shop in Limhamn to my colleagues in Malmö for the time being."

"It wasn't me."

"I heard you say that."

"Can I go now?"

"Yes, you can."

He accompanied her to reception.

"I liked them," she said before leaving. "Both Grandad

111

and Grandma. They were odd people, both secretive and open at the same time. I just wish I could have spent more time with them than turned out to be possible."

Wallander watched her walk away in her high-heeled boots. It occurred to him that she was somebody he would never meet again in this life. But not somebody he would forget all about.

Shortly before twelve he talked briefly to Martinson and Lindman. He explained that the lead had gone cold. They could drop it and move on. Then he informed the prosecutor.

Wallander took the rest of the day off. He bought a new shirt in a shop down in the square, had a pizza at the restaurant next door, then went home to Mariagatan.

When Linda came in that evening, he was already asleep.

CHAPTER 20

The following day was a clear December day with glittering sunshine. Wallander got up early and went for a long walk by the sea before deciding at eight o'clock that it was time to become a police officer again, and headed for the station. They would be forced to take a step backward, and restart the investigation where they had left it when the Simon Larsson lead cropped up.

Before he got down to business, however, there was a telephone call he needed to make. He looked up the number. It rang several times before anybody answered.

"Larsson."

"It's Wallander. Nice to see you the other day."

"Ditto."

"I just wanted to tell you that we've looked into

the information you gave us—but there was a natural explanation. Would you like me to tell you what it was?"

"I'm interested, of course."

Wallander spelled it out. Simon Larsson listened in silence.

"Well, at least I now know what really happened," he said. "I'm sorry I landed you with unnecessary work."

"Nothing is unnecessary," said Wallander. "You know what being a police officer involves. In many cases it is just as important to eliminate leads as it is to find them."

"Maybe that's the way it was. But I'm so old now that I don't remember much of my time in the police."

"There's nothing wrong with your memory. You've proved that already."

Wallander could feel that Simon Larsson wanted to continue talking. Even though they had no more to say, he kept the conversation going. Wallander thought of the woman he had seen lying asleep on top of the bed.

He eventually managed to end the call, and couldn't help wondering what growing old entailed. How would he manage it himself? Becoming ancient and unable to stop talking?

At nine o'clock they assembled in the conference room.

"We'll have to start up again where we finished," said Wallander. "There is a solution to this mystery, even if we can't see it at the moment."

"I agree with you," said Martinson. "Sweden is a small

country, but it has unusually good records of the people who live here. It was the same sixty years ago, even
if people then didn't have the personal numbers that
accompany us from the cradle to the grave. Somebody
must have missed those people. Somebody must have
asked after them."

Wallander had an idea.

"You're right. Somebody ought to have missed them.
Two middle-aged people who disappeared. But if we
think that nobody actually did miss them after all, that
nobody did ask after them—surely that's meaningful in
itself?"

"Nobody misses them because nobody knows they
went missing?"

"Possibly. It could just as well be that somebody did
in fact miss them—but not here."

"Now you've lost me."

Stefan Lindman joined in the conversation.

"You're thinking about the Second World War. We
spoke about it earlier. Skåne was an isolated province,
surrounded by countries at war. British and German
bombers made emergency landings here in our fields,
refugees arrived from all over the place."

"Something like that, yes," said Wallander. "I don't
want us to jump to conclusions too soon. I just want us
to keep all our options open. There are lots of possible
explanations, not just those that our experience tells us

are the most likely ones. There might also be an explanation that we haven't really thought of yet. That's all I meant."

"It wasn't all that unusual for people to earn a bit of extra cash by looking after and letting rooms to refugees."

"Who paid?"

"The refugees had their own organizations. People who had money helped those who hadn't. It produced some extra income for farmers—especially as they probably didn't pay any tax on it."

Martinson reached for a file lying on the table.

"We've received an additional report from Stina Hurlén," he said. "Nothing that changes anything we know already. The only thing is she says that the woman had bad teeth while the man's were more or less perfect."

"Do you think there are dental records that go that far back?"

"That wasn't what I was thinking about. Nor was Stina Hurlén. It was merely a statement of fact. One of the skulls had lots of mended teeth, the other one had perfect teeth. That also tells a story, even if we don't know what it is."

Wallander noted down the information about the teeth on a sheet of paper in his file.

"Has she written anything else?"

"Nothing that seems significant just now. The man had broken his arm at some point. His left arm. That might be helpful to know if we get close to identifying them."

"Not if," said Wallander. "When. In any case, we must find out how things stand with old dental records."

They ran through all the investigation material one more time. There were a lot of possibilities that they hadn't yet started to look into. They broke up as lunchtime approached, having made plans for the next few days.

Martinson had more to say to Wallander after Stefan Lindman had left.

"What about the house? What shall we do about that?"

"It doesn't seem very important just now. As I'm sure you understand."

"Of course. But I thought you should have a bit more time. My wife agrees with me. It could be that you'll view things differently once we've identified the skeletons, all being well."

Wallander shook his head.

"I think you should look for another buyer," he said. "I wouldn't be able to live in a place that's probably the scene of a crime. Nothing can change that, even if we manage to solve the case."

"Are you sure?"

"Absolutely certain."

Martinson seemed disappointed. But he said nothing, merely left the room. Wallander opened a bottle of mineral water and sat with his feet up on the table.

He had been on the point of buying a house. But his vision of the house had been undermined by two dead bodies that had been lying in the ground for many years, and now had come up to the surface.

He wished the house had not been a troll that had suddenly been transformed when exposed to sunlight.

He couldn't remember when he had last felt as listless as he did now. What was it due to? Was it the disappointment that he couldn't manage to shake off? Or was it something else?

CHAPTER 21

Many years ago Wallander had learned that one of the manifold virtues a police officer must possess is the ability to be patient with himself. There would always be days when nothing happened, when an investigation had become bogged down and refused to move either forward or backward. All one could do then was to be patient, and wait until a way of solving the problem emerged. It was easy for police officers to become impatient. They could work fast and with great enthusiasm, but they must never become impatient on days when nothing happened.

Two days passed when nothing happened—not on the surface, at least. Wallander and his colleagues dug deeper and deeper into various archives, searching in basements like animals digging underground passages through the darkness. Occasionally they met over coffee to report on how far they had got, then returned to their own little hideaway.

Outside the police station the weather seemed unable to make up its mind if it was going to be winter or not. One day it was cold, with snowflakes fluttering to the ground; the next day it was plus temperatures again and relentless rain drifted in from the Baltic.

It was a few minutes past nine in the morning on December 6 when the telephone on Wallander's over-loaded desk rang. He gave a start, and picked up the receiver. At first he didn't recognize the voice. It belonged to a woman who spoke with a very marked Scanian accent.

Then he realized that the person he was speaking to was somebody he had met recently. It was Katja Blomberg.

"I've been thinking," she said. "Thinking and thinking, ever since I spoke to you. And then I read about the missing persons. That was when something struck me. The chest in the attic."

"I'm afraid I don't quite follow you."

"I've kept everything I inherited from my grandparents in an old chest. It's been standing in the attic ever since they died. I thought I recognized the name Ludvig Hansson: it was his house they burgled. Then I looked again in the old chest. I haven't done that for many years.

There were quite a lot of diaries in a box in there. Or perhaps I ought to call them almanacs. They belonged to Ludvig Hansson. I thought they might be something you ought to take a look at."

"Almanacs?"

"He noted down when he sowed and when he harvested. He recorded the price he had to pay for things. But he also wrote about a few other things as well."

"What things?"

"About his family and friends, and people who came to visit him."

Wallander started to become interested.

"So he kept these almanacs during the war years, did he?"

"Yes."

"I'd certainly like to look at them. Preferably without delay."

"I could call in right away if you'd like me to."

An hour later Katja Blomberg was sitting at his desk again, smoking. On the desk in front of her was an old wooden box.

The box contained almanacs with black leather covers. The year was printed in gold on the front cover of each. Ludvig Hansson had written his name on the title pages. There were four almanacs, dated 1941, 1942, 1943 and 1944. The box also contained some old bills. Wallander put on his glasses and started leafing through the almanacs. He started with the one for 1941 and worked through the rest. Sure enough, there was information about sowing and harvesting, a broken plow and a horse that "died mysteriously on September 12." There were records about cows and volumes of milk, the slaughter of pigs and the selling of eggs. Occasionally Ludvig Hansson made notes about extreme temperatures. A week in December 1943 had been "hellish cold," while July 1942 was so dry that Hansson "despaired about the harvest."

Wallander read. He noted that various people's birthdays were celebrated, and occasionally there were funerals that were either "painful" or "too long." All the time Katja sat there, chain-smoking.

Wallander moved on to the last of the almanacs, the one for 1944, without feeling that he had become better acquainted with Ludvig Hansson; neither had he found any details that could throw light on the discovery of the skeletons.

But suddenly he paused at the entry for May 12, 1944. Hansson had noted down that "the Estonians have arrived. Three of them: father, mother and son. Kaarin, Elmo and Ivar Pihlak. An advance has been paid." Wallander frowned. Who were these Estonians? What had been paid in advance, and why? He continued reading slowly. Another note on August 14 said: "payments on time again. The Estonians pleasant and cause no trouble. Good business." What exactly had been good business? He continued reading.

It was not until November 20 that there was another note—and it was the last one. "They have left. Accommodation a mess."

Wallander looked through the loose papers in the box without finding anything of note.

"I need to keep these almanacs," he said. "You can have the box back, of course."

"Was there anything of interest?" Katja Blomberg asked.

"Perhaps. In 1944 an Estonian family appears to have been living there. Between May 12 and the end of November."

Wallander thanked her, and left the almanacs lying on the desk. Could this be the solution? he wondered. An Estonian family living at the farm in 1944. But they leave, they don't die. Ludvig Hansson can hardly have killed them.

Martinson was about to go and eat when Wallander came to his office. Wallander asked him to delay his lunch. Stefan Lindman was too busy ferreting away in some of the endless registers and archives. They sat down in Martinson's office. Wallander did the talking while Martinson leafed through the almanacs.

Wallander finished his account of what he had discovered. Martinson seemed doubtful.

"It doesn't seem all that credible."

"It's the first bit of new concrete information we have."

"Three people. A whole family. We've found two skeletons. Nyberg is sure that there aren't any more."

"There could be another body buried somewhere else."

"If we assume that they were staying in Sweden illegally, or in secret, it won't be so easy to track them down."

"Even so, we've got some names. Three names. Kaarin, Elmo and Ivar Pihlak. I'm going to look into them anyway, and see if we can come up with anything."

Martinson stood up and prepared to leave for his delayed lunch.

"If I were you I'd start with the annual census," he said. "Even if it's not all that likely they'll be in it."

"I can't think of any better place to start," said Wallander. "Then we'll see."

Wallander left the police station. He thought he ought to eat. There was a lot he ought to do.

For a brief moment he felt listless again as he sat in the driving seat of his car with the key in his hand. Then he got a grip of himself, switched on the engine and set off to trace the Estonian family.

CHAPTER 22

The woman behind the counter at the local tax office listened sympathetically to what he had to say, but she was not exactly encouraging once she had heard the whole story.

"It will probably be difficult," she said. "We've had people here before looking for traces of people from the Baltic States who had been in Skåne during the war years. You're the first police officer, but there have been others—mainly relatives. We very rarely find them."

"Why's that?"

"Some probably gave false names. Many of them didn't have any identity documents at all when they arrived. But of course the most important reason is that so much has happened in the Baltic States, both during and after the war."

"Have you any idea of how many of these refugees never actually registered?"

"Somebody in Lund wrote a dissertation on that a few years ago. According to the data he uncovered, about seventy-five percent of them actually registered."

She stood up and left the room. Wallander sat down and looked out through the window. He was already wondering how they were going to get any further with this lead. He concluded that they were going to get nowhere.

He was tempted to leave. Get into his car, leave Skåne and never come back. But it was too late for such a drastic move, he knew that. At best, he might one day find the house he was looking for and buy a dog. And perhaps also find a woman who could become the companion he so badly needed. Linda was right. He really was on the way to becoming a lifeless, bitter old codger.

He dismissed all such thought in annoyance, then leaned back in the chair and closed his eyes.

He was woken up by somebody saying his name. When he opened his eyes, the woman was standing there with a sheet of paper in her hand.

"Sometimes it turns out that I'm too pessimistic," she said. "I think I might have found what you're looking for."

Wallander jumped up from his chair.

"Is that really possible?"

"It seems so."

The woman sat down at her desk, and Wallander sat opposite her. She read out from the paper she had in her hand. Wallander noticed that she was farsighted, but she did not use reading glasses.

"Kaarin, Elmo and Ivar Pihlak came to Sweden from Denmark in February 1944," she said. "They lived in Malmö at first. Then they had an apartment in Ludvig Hansson's house, and they were listed as living there in the official national register. In November that same year they requested permission to leave Sweden and return to Denmark. And they duly left Sweden. It's all recorded here."

"How can you be so certain of that?"

"Various special notes were made during the war with regard to refugees. It's their son who notified the authorities of their departure."

Wallander was confused.

"I'm not completely with you. What son?"

"Ivar. He reported that his parents had left Sweden in November 1944."

"What did he do then?"

"He stayed on in Sweden and was granted a residence permit. Later on he became a Swedish citizen. In 1954, to be precise."

Wallander held his breath. He tried to think clearly. Three Estonians come to Sweden in 1944. Father, mother and son. In November that same year the parents go back to Denmark, but the son stays on here. And he's the one who reports that his parents have left Sweden.

"I take it it's not possible to say if the son is still alive. Or if he is, where he might be living."

"I can tell you that, no problem. He's been registered in Ystad for many years. His current address is recorded as Ekudden. That's an old people's home not far from the old prison."

Wallander knew where it was.

"So he's still alive, is he?"

"Yes. He's eighty-six years old, but he's still alive."

Just for a moment Wallander stared out into space. Then he left the room.

CHAPTER 23

On the outskirts of Ystad Wallander stopped at a filling station and had a hot dog. He was still not sure what the information he had received from the tax authorities actually indicated. If, in fact, it indicated anything at all.

He drank some coffee served in a plastic mug before continuing on his way.

Ekudden was just off the main road to Trelleborg—a large, old building in extensive grounds, with views of the sea and the entrance to Ystad harbor. Wallander parked his car and went through the gate. A few elderly men were playing boules on one of the gravel paths. Wallander entered the building, gave a friendly nod to two old ladies who sat knitting, and knocked on a door with a sign saying "Office." A woman in her thirties opened the door.

"My name's Wallander and I'm a police officer here in Ystad."

"I know your daughter, Linda," said the woman with a smile. "We went to the same school a long time ago. I was in your flat in Mariagatan once when you came in through the door: I remember being scared to death!"

"Of me?"

"Of you, yes! You were so enormously big."

"I don't think I'm all that big, am I? Do you know that Linda has come back to Ystad?"

"Yes, I bumped into her in the street. I know she's become a police officer."

"Do you think she seems frightening now?"

The girl laughed. She had a name tag pinned to her blouse: she was evidently called Pia.

"I have a question," said Wallander. "I've been told that a man called Ivar Pihlak lives here."

"Yes, Ivar lives here. He has a room on the first floor, right at the end of the corridor."

"Is he at home?"

Pia looked at him in surprise.

"It's very seldom that the old folks who live here are not at home."

"Do you know if he has any relatives?"

"He's never had any visitors. I don't think he has a family. His parents live in Estonia. Or lived, rather. I seem to recall that he once said they were dead, and that he doesn't have any relatives left."

"How is he?"

"He's eighty-six years old. He can think clearly, but he's a bit limited physically. Why do you want to meet him?"

"It's just a routine matter."

Wallander suspected Pia didn't believe him. Not a hundred percent, at least. She ushered him to the staircase and accompanied him up to the first floor.

The door to Ivar Pihlak's room was ajar. She knocked.

Sitting at a little table in front of a window was an elderly man with white hair, playing patience. He looked up and smiled.

"You have a visitor," said Pia.

"What a nice surprise!" said the man.

Wallander could hear no trace of a foreign accent in his voice.

"I'll leave you to it," said Pia.

She went back along the corridor. The old man had stood up. They shook hands. He smiled: his eyes were blue and his grip was firm.

It seemed to Wallander that everything was wrong. The man standing in front of him would never be able to supply him with a solution to the riddle of the two skeletons.

"I didn't catch your name," said Ivar Pihlak.

"My name's Kurt Wallander and I'm a police officer. For a while during the war, many years ago, you and your parents lived on a farm just outside Löderup that belonged to a man called Ludvig Hansson. You lived there for just over six months, and then your parents went back to Denmark but you stayed on here in Sweden. Is that right?"

"How amazing that you should come here and talk about that now! After so many years."

Ivar Pihlak looked at him with his blue eyes. It was as if Wallander's words had both surprised him and awoken melancholic memories.

"So it's true, is it?"

"My parents went back to Denmark in the beginning of December 1944. The war was coming to an end. They had a lot of friends—there were lots of other Estonians in Denmark. I suppose they didn't really feel at home in Sweden."

"Can you tell me exactly what happened?"

"Might I ask why you're so interested?"

Wallander thought it over and decided not to mention the skeletons.

"It's just a routine matter. Nothing special. What happened?"

"My parents returned to Estonia in June 1945. To their home in Tallinn. It was partially ruined, but they began to rebuild it."

"But you stayed here in Sweden, is that right?"

"I didn't want to go back. I stayed on here. I've never regretted it. I was able to train to become an engineer."

"Do you have any family?"

"It never happened, I'm afraid. That's something I regret, now that I'm an old man."

"Did your parents come to visit you here?"

"It was usually a case of me going to Estonia. Things were very difficult there after the war, as you know."

"When did your parents die?"

"My mother died as early as 1965, my father in the eighties."

"What happened to their home?"

"An uncle on my father's side took care of everything. I was there for their funerals. I brought some of their belongings back here to Sweden with me. But I got rid of everything when I moved in here. There's not a lot of room for stuff here as you can see."

Wallander felt he had no more questions to ask. The whole situation was pointless. The man with the blue eyes looked directly at him all the time, and spoke in a calm, soft voice.

"I won't disturb you anymore," said Wallander. "Good-bye, and many thanks."

Wallander walked back through the garden. The men were still playing boules. Wallander paused and watched them. Something had begun to worry him. At first he couldn't pin it down, apart from being aware that it had to do with the conversation he had had with the old man a few minutes earlier.

Then the penny dropped. It was as if the man's

responses had been rehearsed. No matter what he had asked, he received an answer—a little too fast, a little too precisely.

I'm imagining things, Wallander thought. I'm seeing ghosts where there aren't any ghosts.

He drove back to the police station. Linda was sitting in the canteen, drinking coffee. He sat down at her table. There were a few ginger biscuits on a plate, and he ate them all.

"How's it going?" she asked.

"It's not going at all," he said. "We're standing still."

"Will you be at home for dinner this evening?"

"I think so."

She stood up and returned to her duties. Wallander finished his coffee and then went to his office.

The afternoon slid slowly past.

Just as he was about to go home, the telephone rang.

CHAPTER 24

He recognized her voice, even before she had a chance to give her name. It was the girl called Pia on the telephone.

"I didn't know where I should ring to reach you," she said.

"What's happened?"

"Ivar has disappeared."

"What exactly do you mean by that?"

"He's disappeared. He's run away."

Wallander sat down at his desk. He noticed that his heart was beating faster.

"Calm down," he said. "Tell me bit by bit. What's happened?"

"He didn't come down for dinner an hour ago. So I went up to his room. It was empty. His jacket was missing. We looked for him in the building and in the garden and down on the beach. He wasn't anywhere to be found. Then Miriam came and said that her car was missing."

"Who's Miriam?"

"She works here, her job is identical to mine. She thought Ivar might have taken her car."

"Why should Ivar have taken it?"

"She doesn't usually lock her car. And Ivar often talked about how much he used to like driving."

"What make of car does she have?"

"A dark blue Fiat."

Wallander noted that down. Then he thought for a moment.

"Are you certain that Ivar isn't in the house or the garden?"

"We've looked everywhere."

"Why do you think he's run away?"

"I thought you would be able to explain that."

"I know where he might be. I'm not sure, but I might be right. If I find him I'll be in touch within an hour or so. If I don't find him I'll have to make it an official police matter. Then we shall have to work out the best way of starting some kind of organized search."

Wallander hung up. He sat motionless on his chair. Was he right? Had that uneasiness he had felt earlier been founded on fact?

He stood up. It was 5:35. It was dark outside. The wind came and went in gusts.

CHAPTER 25

Even from a distance Wallander could see that there was a faint light in one of the windows. There was no longer any doubt. His suspicion had been correct. Ivar Pihlak had come to the house where he had once lived with his parents.

Wallander drove onto the shoulder and switched off the engine. Apart from that faint light in the window, everything around him was dark. He picked up the flashlight that he always kept under the driver's seat, and started walking. The wind was lashing at his face. When he reached the house he saw that two lamps in the living room were lit. A kitchen window was broken, and the hasps unfastened. Pihlak had placed a garden chair so that he could climb in. Wallander looked in through the window but could see no sign of him. He decided to enter the house the same way as Pihlak, through the broken kitchen window. He didn't think he needed to be worried. The man inside the house was old—an old man whose fate had caught up with him.

Wallander climbed in. He stood motionless on the kitchen floor and listened. He regretted that he had driven out to the farm alone. He felt in his jacket pocket for his cell phone, then remembered that he had put it down on the car seat when he had been feeling for the flashlight. He tried to make a decision. Should he stay where he was, or climb out through the window again and ring for Martinson? He opted for the latter, squeezed out through the window and started walking toward the car.

Whether it was an instinctive reaction or if he had heard a noise behind him was something he could never work out afterward, but something hit him on the back of his head before he had time to turn around. Everything went black before he hit the ground.

When he came around he was sitting on a chair. His trousers and shoes were covered in mud. A dull pain was nagging away inside his head.

Standing in front of him was Ivar Pihlak. He had a gun in his hand. An old German army–issue pistol, Wallander could see. Pihlak's eyes were still blue, but the smile had disappeared. He simply looked tired. Tired, and very old.

Wallander started thinking. Pihlak had been out there

in the darkness and had knocked him out. Then the old man had dragged him into the house. Wallander glanced at his watch: half past six. So he hadn't been unconscious for very long.

He tried to assess the situation. The gun aimed at him was dangerous, despite the fact that the man holding it was eighty-six years old. Wallander must not underestimate Ivar Pihlak. He had knocked him out, and earlier in the day he had stolen a car and driven out to Löderup.

Wallander felt scared. Speak calmly, he told himself quietly. Speak perfectly calmly, listen, don't complain; simply speak and listen very calmly.

"Why did you come?" asked Pihlak.

His voice sounded sorrowful again, as Wallander had thought it sounded at Ekudden. But he was also tense.

"Why did I come here, or why did I go to where you live?"

"Why did you come? I'm an old man and I shall soon be dead. I don't want to feel anxious. I've been anxious all my life."

"All I want is to understand what happened," said Wallander slowly. "A few weeks ago I came out here to look at this house. Possibly to buy it. And then, purely by chance, I stumbled upon a piece of a skeleton, a hand, in the garden."

"It's not true," said Pihlak.

He suddenly sounded irascible and impatient; his voice had become falsetto. Wallander held his breath.

"You lot have always been after me," said Pihlak. "You've been chasing after me for sixty years. Why can't I be left in peace? I mean, all that's left is the epilogue: the fact that I shall die."

"It was pure coincidence. We're just trying to find out who it was that died."

"That's not true. You want to put me in prison. You want me to die in a prison cell."

"In Sweden all crimes are statute-barred after twenty-five years. Nothing will happen to you, no matter what you say."

Pihlak pulled a chair toward him and sat down. All the time the pistol was pointed at Wallander.

"I promise not to do anything," said Wallander. "You're welcome to tie me up if you want. But put that pistol away."

Pihlak said nothing. He kept the gun pointing steadily at Wallander's head.

"I was afraid all those years, of course—afraid that you would find me," he said after awhile.

"Have you ever been back here? During all those years?"

"Never."

"Never?"

"Not a single time. I studied to become an engineer at the Chalmers technical university in Gothenburg. Then I worked for an engineering company in Örnsköldsvik until the mid-sixties. Then I moved back to Gothenburg and worked at the Eriksberg shipyard for a few years. Then I went to Malmö—but never here. Never ever. Until I moved into Ekudden."

Wallander could hear that the man was beginning to hold forth. It was the beginning of the tale he wanted to tell. Wallander tried to surreptitiously change his posture so that the pistol was no longer pointing straight at his face.

"Why couldn't you leave me in peace?"

"We have to find out who those dead people are. That's what the police do."

Ivar Pihlak suddenly burst out laughing.

"I never thought they would be discovered. Not during my lifetime, at least. But they were. Earlier today you stood there in the doorway and started asking me questions. Tell me what you know."

"We found two skeletons, a man and a woman. Both in their fifties. They've been lying there for at least fifty years. Both had been killed. That's all."

"That's not much."

"There's one more thing I know. The woman had a lot of fillings in her teeth, but the man's teeth were quite different."

Pihlak nodded slowly. "He was tightfisted. Not with himself, but with everybody else."

"Are you referring to your father?"

"Who else would I be talking about?"

"I ask questions I need answers to. Nothing else."

"He was so incredibly mean. And evil. He wouldn't let her go to the dentist until her teeth had started to rot away. He treated my mother as if she were totally devoid of dignity. He used to humiliate her by waking her up in the middle of the night, forcing her to lie naked on the floor and repeat over and over again how worthless she was, until dawn. She was so scared of him that she started shaking whenever he was near."

Ivar Pihlak suddenly fell silent. Wallander waited. The gun was still pointing straight at him. Wallander had the feeling that this trial of strength could last awhile. But he had to wait for the moment when the man lost concentration. Then Wallander would have the opportunity of attacking him and taking away his gun.

"During those years I often wondered about my mother," said Pihlak. "Why couldn't she simply leave him? It made me both despise her and feel sorry for her. How can you possibly have such contrasting feelings for the same person? I still haven't found a satisfactory answer to that. But if she had left him, it would never have happened."

Wallander suspected there was deep-seated anguish in everything Ivar Pihlak said. But he still wasn't sure what caused that feeling.

"One day she'd had enough," said Pihlak. "She hanged herself in the kitchen. I couldn't take any more . . ."

"So you killed him?"

"It was during the night. I must have woken up when

she kicked the chair away. But my father carried on sleeping peacefully. I hit him on the head with a hammer. I dug the graves that same night. By dawn they were already buried and the surface soil had been replaced."

"But some of the currant bushes ended up in the wrong place."

Pihlak looked at Wallander in surprise.

"Is that how you caught on to it?"

"What happened next?"

"It was all straightforward. I reported that they had both left Sweden. Nobody checked up on that information: the war was still on, everything was in chaos, people were fleeing all over the place, without identities, without roots, without aims. And so I moved, first to Sjöbo, and then, after the war, to Gothenburg. I lived in various apartments while I was studying. I supported myself by working in the docks. I had strong arms in those days."

The gun was still pointing at Wallander, but he had the feeling that Ivar Pihlak's concentration was less intense. Wallander cautiously moved his feet so that when the moment came he would be able to brace himself before throwing himself at the old man.

"My father was a monster," said Pihlak. "I have never regretted what I did. But I was unable to avoid my punishment. I see his shadow around me all the time. I think I see my father's face and hear him saying: 'You will never be able to shake me off.'"

He suddenly burst into tears. Wallander hesitated,

but realized the moment had come. He jumped up off the chair and threw himself at Ivar Pihlak—but he had misjudged the old man's alertness. He swayed to one side and hit Wallander on the head with the butt of his pistol. It was not a hard blow, but it was sufficient to knock Wallander out. When he came back to his senses, Pihlak was leaning over him.

"You should have left me alone," Pihlak yelled. "You should have let me die with my shame and my secret. That was all I asked. But now you've come and ruined everything."

Wallander was horrified to note that Pihlak had now passed beyond his limit. He would shoot at any moment. Trying to attack him again was bound to fail.

"I'll leave you in peace," said Wallander. "I understand why you did what you did. I shall never say anything."

"It's too late. Why should I believe you? You threw yourself at me. You thought you'd be able to sort out an old codger like me without any difficulty."

"I don't want to die."

"Nobody does. But we all do in the end."

Ivar Pihlak took a step toward him. He was holding the gun with both hands now. Wallander wanted to close his eyes, but he didn't dare. Linda's face flitted past in his mind's eye.

Pihlak pulled the trigger. But no bullet hit Wallander. No bullet emerged at all. When Ivar Pihlak pulled the trigger, the gun exploded. Bits of metal from the ancient pistol hit Pihlak in the forehead, making a deep hole, and he was dead before his body hit the floor.

Wallander sat there for ages without moving. He felt incomprehensibly happy inside. He was alive, but the old man was dead. The gun Ivar Pihlak had held in his hands had not obeyed him during the last second of his life.

Wallander eventually stood up and staggered out to his car. He phoned Martinson and told him what had happened.

He remained outside the house, buffeted by the wind, waiting. He was thinking of nothing, and he wanted nothing. Being able to continue living was quite enough.

It was fourteen minutes before he saw the first of the blue lights approaching.

CHAPTER 26

Two weeks later, a few days before Christmas, Linda accompanied her father to the farm in Löderup. She had insisted that he should pay the place one more visit, then he could give the keys back to Martinson and begin looking seriously for another house.

It was a cold, clear day. Wallander said nothing, and had his cap pulled down low over his forehead. Linda wanted him to show her where Ivar Pihlak had died, and where her father had also thought death had come to collect him. Wallander pointed and mumbled, but when Linda wanted to ask questions he merely shook his head. There was nothing else to say.

Afterward they drove back to Ystad, and went to a pizzeria for a meal. Immediately after the food had been served Wallander started to feel sick. It was a sudden attack, and seemed to come from nowhere. He just managed to get into the men's room before it was too late.

Linda looked at him in surprise when he came back. "Are you ill?"

"I suppose it's only just dawned on me how close I was to dying."

He could see that the reality of it all had only just dawned on her as well. They sat there in silence for a long time. The food went cold. It occurred to Wallander later that they had hardly ever been as close to each other as they were at that time.

The following morning Wallander went early to the police station. He knocked on the door of Martinson's office. There was nobody there. From another room he could hear the sound of Christmas carols on the radio. Wallander went into the room and put the house keys on Martinson's desk.

Then he left the police station and walked down to the center of town. It was snowing—wet snow that melted and formed slush on the pavements.

Wallander stopped outside the biggest real estate agent's in town. The windows were covered with pictures of houses for sale between Ystad and Simrishamn.

Wallander blew his nose into his fingers. There was a house just outside Kåseberga that interested him.

He went in. As he did so all thoughts of Ivar Pihlak and his story faded into memory. They might come to haunt him in the future, but they would always remain no more than a memory.

Wallander leafed through catalogues and examined photographs of various houses.

He lost interest in the house he had seen in the window, the one just outside Kåseberga. The plot was too small, the neighboring houses were too close. He continued looking through the catalogues. There were a lot of houses and farms to choose from, but the price was usually too high. Perhaps an underpaid police officer is condemned to live in an apartment, he thought ironically.

But he had no intention of giving up. He would find that house one day, and he would buy a dog. Next year he would leave Mariagatan for good. He had made up his mind.

The day after Wallander's first visit to the real estate agent's, there was a thin white layer of snow over the town and the brown fields.

Christmas that year was cold. Icy winds blew over Skåne from the Baltic.

Winter had arrived early.

AFTERWORD

This story was written many years ago. It had been decided in Holland that everybody who bought a crime novel in a certain month would receive a free book. I was asked if I would write a story. It was a good idea—making people more interested in reading.

The book was duly published. Many years later the BBC discovered the story and made it the basis of a manuscript for a television film in which Kenneth Branagh would play the part of Wallander. I saw the film, and realized that the story still felt alive and relevant.

Later, when it became necessary to make a list of all my Wallander stories, I saw an opportunity to publish this "Dutch" story once again.

Chronologically, it dates to the period just before *The Troubled Man*, which completed the Wallander series. There are no more stories about Kurt Wallander.

Henning Mankell
Gothenburg, October 2012

MANKELL ON WALLANDER

HOW IT STARTED, HOW IT FINISHED AND WHAT HAPPENED IN BETWEEN

In a cardboard box down in my cellar is a collection of dusty diaries. They go back quite a long way in time. I've been keeping a diary since about 1965. Regularly on and off, you might say. They contain all kinds of things from attempts to create aphorisms to straightforward notes reminding me about things I'd prefer not to have forgotten about the following day. They contain a lot of gaps, sometimes a month or more long, but there are also periods when I have written every day.

Such as in the spring of 1990. I had returned from a long, unbroken stay in Africa, where I lived for six months at a time. When I got home I soon realized that while

I had been away racist tendencies had started to spread in Sweden in a most unpleasant way. Sweden has never been totally free from this social evil, but it was obvious to me that it had increased dramatically.

After a few months, I made up my mind to write about racism. I had quite different plans at the time for what I was going to write about, but I thought this was important.

More important.

When I began to think about what kind of story it would be, it soon dawned on me that the natural path to follow was a crime novel. This was obvious because in my world racist acts are criminal outrages. A logical consequence of this was that I would need an investigator, a crime expert, a police officer.

One day in May 1990 I wrote in my diary—unfortunately more or less illegible for anyone but me: *The warmest day this spring. Went for a walk round the fields. A lot of bird-song. It seemed to me that the police officer I shall describe must realize how difficult it is to be a good police officer. Crime changes in the same way that a society changes. If he is going to be able to do his work properly, he must understand what is going on in the society he lives in.*

I was living in Skåne at the time, in the middle of what could be called "Wallanderland." I lived in a farmhouse on the edge of the village of Trunnerup. From the garden I could see the sea and a lot of church towers and steeples. When I got back from my walk I took out the telephone directory. First I found the name Kurt. It was short and sounded fairly usual. A longer surname would be appropriate. I spent quite a while looking, and eventually hit upon Wallander.

That was also neither too common, nor too uncommon.

So that was what my police officer would be called: Kurt Wallander. And I let him be born in the same year as me: 1948. (Some pedants maintain that this isn't consistently true in all the books. I'm sure they are right. What is consistently true in this life?)

Everything one writes is part of a tradition. Authors who maintain that they are totally divorced from literary traditions are lying. You don't become an artist in no-man's-land.

When I started thinking about how *Faceless Killers* should be written, I realized that the best and most fundamental "crime stories" I could think of were classical Greek dramas. The tradition goes back more than two thousand years in time. A play like *Medea*, which is about a woman who murders her children because she is jealous of her husband, reflects human beings through the mirror of crime. It's about contradictions between us and inside us, between individuals and society, between dream and reality. Sometimes these contradictions express themselves in violence, such as racial conflict. And this mirror of crime can take us back to the Greek authors.

They still inspire us. The only real difference between then and now is that in those days there was hardly anything corresponding to our police force. Conflicts were resolved in a different way; often, gods held sway over human destiny. But generally speaking, that is the only basic difference.

The great Danish-Norwegian author Aksel Sandemose once said, liberally translated, "the only things worth writing about are love and murder." He may well have been right. If he had added money, he would have created a trinity, which in one way or another is always present in literature, then as now, and presumably always will be.

I wrote that novel without ever thinking that there might be more featuring Chief Inspector Wallander. But I realized after the book had been published—and even won a prize—that I might have created a set-up that could be developed further. Another book was written, *The Dogs of Riga*, dealing with what happened in Europe after the collapse of the Berlin Wall. I flew to Riga, and afterward often felt that I ought to write a book about those weeks I spent in Latvia. It was a remarkable time. Tensions between Russians and Latvians had not yet reached bursting point. When I wanted to speak to a Latvian police officer it had to be a secret meeting in a dimly lit beer house. Much of the atmosphere in the novel was a gift as far as I was concerned—I merely had to reproduce the difficulties I had in finding my way around with political tensions red-hot on all sides.

But I was still not convinced that there would be a series of novels featuring Kurt Wallander. However, on January 9, 1993, I sat down in my little apartment in Maputo to write a third book. It was to be called *The White Lioness*, and would be about the situation in South Africa. Nelson Mandela had been released from prison some years previously, but there was still a real danger that civil war might break out and plunge the country into chaos. It did not take long to work out that the worst thing that could possibly happen would be for Mandela to be murdered. Nothing could prevent that from leading to a bloodbath.

But just before I actually started writing I became very ill. I had been wandering around Maputo for some time feeling out of sorts. I was tired out, pale, couldn't sleep. Could I be suffering from malaria? But blood tests showed no sign of parasites. Then one day I bumped into a good friend of mine who took one look at me and said:

"Your face is all yellow!"

I don't remember much about being rushed into a hospital in Johannesburg, but once I got there I was diagnosed as suffering from an aggressive type of jaundice, and had been doing so for far too long.

I lay in my hospital bed, working out the story in my mind during the nights. By the time I had recovered sufficiently to travel back home to Maputo, it was more or less ready for writing down. If I remember rightly, I wrote the last page first. That was the point I was working toward!

On April 10 that year, when I had already submitted the text to my publisher, I received worrying confirmation of how my thoughts on the subject had been only too right. On Good Friday a fanatical apartheid supporter shot dead Chris Hani, the chairman of South Africa's Communist Party, and number two in the ANC. There was no civil war, thanks largely to Nelson Mandela's intelligent politics. But I still wonder what would have happened if he had been the victim.

People sometimes say about the Wallander books that they deal with events that later happen in real life. I think that is true. I have no doubt that in some respects it is not impossible to foresee the future, and actually to be right. I thought it went without saying that when the Soviet Union collapsed and the eastern states opened up, we would be plagued by a new kind of criminality in Sweden and Western Europe. And that is what happened.

The starting point for *The Man Who Smiled* is about the worst crime involving property one could possibly commit or be a victim of—and it is not being robbed of one's possessions. What is stolen in such cases is a part of a human being, an organ that can then be sold for transplantation. When I began writing the book I had no doubt that it was a crime that would increase.

Today it is an industry that is flourishing and expanding.

Why did Wallander become so popular in so many different countries and cultures? What exactly was it that made him so many people's friend? It is something I have wondered about, of course, and there is no definite answer. But there might be several partial explanations.

Here is the one I believe in preference to all others!

From the very beginning, when I made that spring walk through the fields, I was clear that I would create a human being who was very like myself and the unknown reader. A person who is constantly changing, both mentally and physically. I am changing all the time, and so he would also do the same.

That led eventually to what I somewhat ironically call "the diabetes syndrome." After the third novel, I asked Victoria, a friend and a doctor who had read the books: "What disease that a lot of people suffer from would you give this man?"

Without a trace of doubt she replied immediately: "Diabetes."

And so the next time I wrote about Wallander, he was diagnosed as having diabetes. And that made him even more popular.

Nobody can imagine James Bond stopping in a street, while chasing after some criminal or other, in order to inject himself with insulin. But Wallander does, and so he becomes like any other person who suffers from that illness, or something similar. He might have been afflicted by rheumatism or gout, a heart with an irregular beat or soaring blood pressure. But in fact he has diabetes, and he still suffers from it, although he has it under control.

Needless to say there are other reasons why Kurt Wallander has attracted so many readers. But I think the fact that he is always changing is crucial. There is a major but simple reason for this: I can only write books that I would want to read myself. And a book in which I either know all there is to know about the main character after just one page, or realize that nothing is going to change him or her in any way for the next thousand pages, is not a book I would have the patience to read.

You attract a lot of friends in the world of art. Sherlock Holmes still receives letters written to him in Baker Street, London. I get letters, e-mails and telephone calls from many countries. I am stopped in the streets of Gothenburg just as often as in Hamburg. The questions people ask me are friendly, and I try to answer them as best I can.

Most of the people who contact me are women who hope to cure Wallander's loneliness. I seldom answer those letters. Nor do I think that the writers expect an answer. People are sensible, despite everything. You can't live with literary characters no matter how much you might like to. You can have them as imaginary friends that you can call up when you need them. One of the tasks of art is to provide people with companions. I have seen people in paintings who I hope to meet in the street one of these days. There are characters in books and films who become so alive that we turn a corner and expect to see them standing there. Wallander is one of those characters who hides behind corners. But he never emerges and shows himself. Not to me, at least.

I was once almost lost for words. It was 1994. There was to be a referendum in Sweden about whether or not we should join the EU. I was walking along Vasagatan in Stockholm when an elderly man stopped by my side. He was very friendly and well mannered, and asked if I was who he thought I was. I said yes. He then asked the following question:

"I wonder if Kurt Wallander will vote for or against the EU?"

His question was serious. I had no reason to doubt that. His curiosity was genuine. But how should I answer? I had never thought about it, of course. I tried desperately to think whether or not I knew if the Swedish police force as a whole was in favor of membership or not. In the end I said: "I think his vote will be the opposite of mine." And I walked away before the friendly man had an opportunity to ask a follow-up question.

On that occasion I voted against membership. And so I am convinced that Wallander voted in favor.

A question I am often asked is what books Wallander reads.

It is a good question, because it is difficult to answer. I sometimes think he reads the books I write. But I'm not entirely convinced.

Unfortunately I don't think Wallander is much of a reader—and what he does read is unlikely to be poetry. But I imagine that he likes reading about history, both factual books and historical novels. And I think he has always been fascinated by books about Sherlock Holmes.

Some people think that what I am about to say is completely untrue. But it is true. It is not a myth. It really did happen.

About fifteen years ago I started writing a book that would have Wallander as the main character. I wrote about a hundred pages, which is the point at which I start to believe seriously that what I am writing is destined to be a book.

But it didn't turn out that way. After a few more pages I gave up and burned—literally—every page that had been printed out. I also erased the computer file, and when I bought a new computer shortly afterward I destroyed the old hard disc. I think I can say with confidence that there are no ones and zeros left that could be used to re-create those hundred pages.

I didn't finish writing the book because I was uncomfortable with it. I didn't have the strength. It was about the abuse of children. Now, of course, I realize that I ought to have written it. Child abuse is one of the most unpleasant crimes in the world nowadays. And Sweden is no exception. But that is precisely why I became so uncomfortable with it. I simply couldn't cope.

I understand that people query the truth of what I have just maintained. I have described a lot of things in my books that could certainly be considered horrendous. And I have no hesitation in saying that I found it extremely difficult to put a lot of pages down on paper. But of course I am aware that what happens in everyday life is always much worse than what I describe in my books. My imagination can never exceed reality. And so, sometimes, I must also write about disgusting things so as not to become divorced from credibility.

After *The White Lioness*, I realized that the Wallander phenomenon was something I could exploit to make the most of what I had to say. At the same time I also realized that I needed to be afraid of the character I had created. From now on there would always be a danger of my forgetting to write my novels to be performed by a full orchestra, and instead to concentrate on his horn solos. What I always needed to bear in mind was: the story is the most important thing. Always. And then to ask myself if Wallander would be a suitable solo instrument to enhance this particular story, or not.

Over and over again I would tell myself: now I'm going to do something different. I wrote texts in which he didn't appear—novels that were not about crimes, plays for the theater. Then I could return to him, drop him, write something different, then return to him again.

All the time I could hear a voice deep down inside me saying: "You must make sure that you drop him at the right moment." I was well aware that one day I might pick up Wallander, stare hard at him and ask myself: "What can I think of for him to do now?" A point when he rather than the story was the most important ingredient. That would be the time to drop him. I think I can say in all honesty that Wallander has never been more important than the actual story.

Wallander never became a burden.

But there was also another warning alarm ticking away inside me. I must avoid starting to write as a sort of routine. If I did that, I would have been caught in a dangerous trap. It would be showing insufficient respect for both my readers and myself. If that happened, readers would pay good money for a book and soon discover that the author had grown tired and was simply going through the motions. As far as I was concerned, my writing would have been transformed into something to which I was no longer fully committed.

And so I stopped while it was still fun. The decision to write my last book about Wallander crept up on me slowly. It was a few years before I was ready to write the final full stop.

It was actually my wife Eva who wrote that final full stop. I had written the last word, and I asked her to press the "full stop" key. She did so, and the story was finished.

And what now, afterward? When I am working on totally different books? I am often asked if I miss Wallander. I answer truthfully. "I'm not the one who will miss him. It's the reader."

I never think about Wallander. For me he is somebody who exists in my head. The three actors who have played him on the television and in films have portrayed their own highly individual versions in brilliant fashion. It has been a great joy for me.

But I don't miss him. And I didn't repeat the mistake made by Sir Arthur Conan Doyle, who halfheartedly killed off Mr. Holmes. That last Sherlock Holmes story is one of the least successful. Presumably because deep down, Doyle was doing something that he knew he would regret.

I am occasionally stopped in the street and asked if I'm not going to write another one, despite everything. And what will happen to his daughter Linda who also became a police officer? Didn't I once say she was going to play the leading role? Didn't I write the first book about her, *Before the Frost*, ten years ago?

I don't want to exclude the possibility that there might be one or possibly even several books in which Linda Wallander plays the leading role, but I am not sure. At my age, the limits of what I can do have narrowed. As always, time is short—but more scarce now than it has ever been. I have to make increasingly definite decisions about what I shall *not* do. That is the only way to use the time I have—and nobody knows how long that is—to do what I want to do most of all.

But I don't regret a single line of the thousands of lines I wrote about Wallander. I think the books live on because in many ways they are a reflection of what happened in Sweden and in Europe in the 1990s and the first decade of the twenty-first century. They are novels of Swedish unrest, as I used to call the series of books about Wallander. How long the texts will continue to live on depends on quite different factors. On what happens in the world, and what happens to reading habits.

The passage of time is in many ways bewildering. I wrote at least half of the first Wallander book on an old Halda typewriter. Nowadays I can hardly remember what tapping the keys of a typewriter was like.

The book world is changing dramatically. It always has done, but one should bear in mind that it is the *distribution* of books that is changing, not the books themselves. The basic idea of reading a book is holding in your hands two covers containing pages. To be sure, more and more people are going to bed with their e-readers, but traditional books with paper pages will never disappear. Without being reactionary in any way, I am convinced that more and more people will go back to reading traditional books.

Whether or not I am right, only time will tell.

In any case, my story about Kurt Wallander has now come to an end. Wallander will soon retire and cease to be a police officer. He will wander around in his twilight land with his black dog Jussi. How much longer he will remain in the land of the living, I have no idea. That is presumably something he will decide for himself.

Henning Mankell
Spring 2013

ALSO BY
HENNING MANKELL

THE TROUBLED MAN

A retired navy officer has vanished in a forest near Stockholm. Kurt Wallander is prepared to stay out of the relatively straightforward investigation—which is, after all, another detective's responsibility—but the missing man is his daughter's father-in-law. With his typical disregard for rules and regulations, Wallander is soon pursuing his own brand of dogged detective work on someone else's case. His methods are often questionable, but the results are not: he finds an extremely complex situation that may involve the secret police and ties back to Cold War espionage.

Crime Fiction

ALSO AVAILABLE
The Pyramid
Faceless Killers
The Dogs of Riga
The White Lioness
The Man Who Smiled
Sidetracked
The Fifth Woman
One Step Behind
Firewall
The Return of the Dancing Master
Before the Frost
Kennedy's Brain
The Man from Beijing
Chronicler of the Winds
Depths
The Eye of the Leopard
Italian Shoes
Daniel
A Treacherous Paradise
The Shadow Girls

VINTAGE CRIME/BLACK LIZARD
Available wherever books are sold.
www.weeklylizard.com